THE LOVE OLYMPICS

THE LOVE OLYMPICS

STORIES

CLAIRE WILKSHIRE

BREAKWATER
P.O. Box 2188, St. John's, NL, Canada, A1C 6E6
WWW.BREAKWATERBOOKS.COM

COPYRIGHT © 2021 Claire Wilkshire
ISBN 978-1-55081-908-3

A CIP catalogue record for this book is available from Library and Archives
Canada

We acknowledge the support of the Canada Council for the Arts.
We acknowledge the financial support of the Government of Canada through
the Department of Heritage and the Government of Newfoundland and
Labrador through the Department of Tourism, Culture, Arts and Recreation
for our publishing activities.

PRINTED AND BOUND IN CANADA.

 Canada Council Conseil des arts
for the Arts du Canada Canadä Newfoundland Labrador

Breakwater Books is committed to choosing papers and materials for our
books that help to protect our environment. To this end, this book is printed
on recycled paper that is certified by the Forest Stewardship Council®.

FOR TIM AND SAL,
WITH LOVE AND LOVE
AND MORE LOVE

CONTENTS

MOTHERS

ON LABOUR DAY weekend, mothers across the country mobilize, and you are among them. Mothers arrive in cities where their children attend university; they arrive with rubber gloves and a measuring tape rolled up in an old pair of jeans tucked inside a carry-on; they stand shoulder to shoulder with their smaller (or larger) incarnations, wiping out fridges in apartments to be vacated and hefting industrial-sized packs of toilet paper into shopping carts. They—you—drive giant white rented SUVs to stores and help fill them up. You lie on your backs on filthy student apartment floors, tightening bolts in assemble-it-yourself furniture with cheap screwdrivers while balls of sweat dribble across your face and plop to the blackened boards. You shake the hands of new roommates and offer up good wishes for the semester, thinking Please be kind to my child. You bolster and encourage in the face of cold feet and incipient homesickness; you smile and hug and are brisk and purposeful. You have built an inner fortress against sadness; you have steeled yourself to maintain a fierce, detached cheeriness as you look at your sweet young (very young) person and see a tear run down the side of a nose. You have unpacked boxes you helped to pack two days earlier; you've advised on storage strategies in small spaces; you have swept and folded and sorted and set up; you have paid restaurant bills because the food was all used up at the old place and it has not yet been purchased for the new one. You've wielded a credit card so often you have tennis elbow, and by evening you are exhausted and depleted. The fortress walls have been breached. They've been breached by fatigue, sweat, uncertainty, and the most fervent desire for your young person to be happy, combined with the knowledge that happiness is beyond your purview. When the young person looks sad and afraid and tearful, you too feel sad and afraid; your eyes fill up and the breeziness of a few hours earlier is unrecoverable.

When children visit, when they come back for Thanksgiving or Easter, when they arrive at the airport with tired smiles, wearing clothes that have not smashed against the inside of a washing machine in recent memory, when they sit around the kitchen table like adults (which they are), with their partners, telling tales of adult lives, which they are living (more or less), they have opinions; they know how to do new things, and some of those things you do not yourself know how to do (make a good grain bowl, map bus routes on an app), and now you would like to know how to do them; they are aware of some global political issues that escaped your attention because you were immersed in some other thing last week, and all you can say is The Italian ambassador, no, I didn't hear about that. You wonder how they learned these things about work and ambassadors when you were not there to tell them. They tip kitchen chairs back or hop up on the counter and sit in the corner, swinging their legs and telling funny stories about profs or co-workers whose names and personalities you mostly know by now; you say Oh, *Adrian*—he didn't! as if you knew Adrian, as if you had ever laid eyes on him, which actually you have because you have creeped him on Facebook but no one needs to know that, and it is in any case normal; it is akin to industrial espionage; it is learning things about the other parties involved in the life of your child that you might potentially have cause to know at some future point because the fact that they are not living with you at this moment doesn't mean they are gone forever, lost to you, that you are just a tiresome old fogey prone to repeating yourself and fretting about boring details; you are mildly confident you haven't quite reached that stage yet—in fact, you might at any point be called upon to perform some task involving protection, assistance, possibly heroic action. And knowing what Adrian's all about is the kind of intel that could hypothetically be useful there.

Over the long weekend they burrow into the couch with blankets; they spend the morning watching videos, sending messages, snorting as they point out funny memes to each other; they spend hours gearing up to work on assignments for courses, and you start to wonder if you

should make suggestions—turn off the music, set a timer—
but all of a sudden when the afternoon is already well
underway they slave away for half an hour and suddenly
bingo! the assignment is done; they wonder if they can
defrost something for lunch; after lunch they eat the grapes,
all the grapes; they eat chips; they locate the crackers and
the good cheese; you come into the kitchen when they have
gone out and gather up the plates, the phone chargers, the
half-empty Diet Coke bottles, the bowls with remnants of
cereal or pea soup, mugs with dregs of lemon tea, you rinse
the coffee grounds out of the bottom of the French press
and put the guitar back in its case and fold the throw on the
armchair and load the dishwasher and turn it on; you wipe
down the table and soon comes the thud of the front door
and they are back; their arms circle around you and they are
laughing, you are laughing, they are young and strong and
warm, except for the frozen hands they hold at the back of
your neck to make you squeak, and you put out more food,
you tell them to help themselves, to settle in, to be comfortable, to leave their laundry in a pile in the hall because you'll
throw on a load for them later, and they laugh again because
they don't care about laundry. But really, you would like to
do their laundry. You look at a pair of feet and say Are those
my socks? and a finger is placed on your lips while someone
says Shh. You would like to do whatever would make their
day easier, you want them to feel good here, to want to come
back, to bring their light and their warmth and their smiles
into the house and deposit them everywhere like flotsam,
like little bunches of grapes, close and fat and sweet.

The night before they leave, they traipse into the bedroom while you're in the ensuite with the door open. They drape themselves over your bed, one on top of the comforter and the other underneath, one with limbs all sprawly, the other bunched up for maximal heat conservation; they are gazing up at the ceiling or into the screen of a phone and their words come out in little lazy clumps with long spaces between them as you brush your teeth and wipe your mouth; no one is addressing anyone in particular as you lift the edge of the comforter and crawl in, pushing gently at the nesting one, who shuffles over a little to make room, and you are three-quarters asleep by the time they roll slowly over and brush lips up against your cheek and murmur goodnight; the bed heaves and they pad away to their rooms as you roll into the warm space they've vacated and try to pretend that they are still there, that the alarm won't go off in the middle of the night and set your heart skittering around like a baby goat, that you won't check the departures website and help load their bags into the trunk and wait until they've checked in, just in case, and walk them to the security area and squeeze them tight and turn away quickly, rubbing the back of your hand over your cheek and heading out in the dark to the cold, empty car.

SNOW

THE WEATHER WAS dry, and the nets stayed up on the soccer field until mid-October. The last Wednesday before they moved into the gym, he was running a couple of easy laps to warm up. He saw her from a distance, sitting in the stands, bending forward, a vaguely familiar figure. When he reached that end of the field, he realized she was leaning over one knee to tie the long laces of her cleats.

"Jess?"

"Oh my god! Look at you."

Straight blonde hair pulled back with an elastic. She hopped up and he remembered she wasn't tall. A quick hug, but the teams were being chosen; she ended up with a red bib and his was blue, so they didn't talk again until half-time, when he offered her his water bottle and said people usually went for a beer afterwards at the bowling alley down the road.

He wasn't a natural athlete. Or any kind of athlete,

really. He lacked stamina. But his footwork was improving. On a good day, he'd tuck his chin down in a blizzard of red bibs and slide through them, come out the other side. Then he'd pass off to a teammate near the net and let them take the shot. It was the best feeling, that no one could touch him.

They sat around a long, sticky table with their red faces and sweaty hair, bright jerseys in that cheap material like lightweight plastic mesh, and she slipped into the seat next to him. Jugs and glasses were arriving. He introduced her to the people she hadn't met yet. She reached across the table to shake hands with them.

"Hi, I'm Jessica, I just moved back from Toronto. The rec centre said there was room for another player. Hi Justin. Hi Ashley."

"So how long have you been back?"

"Just a couple weeks."

"And you were there for...?"

"Eight years."

. . . . .

She'd married Chris Mercer, and they had moved away not long afterward. He'd gone to the wedding, along with all the old crowd, in a farmer's field overlooking Middle Cove. A motorcycle roared past, obliterating several lines of Khalil Gibran, and Jess's sister paused, not sure what to do, until someone called out *Start over, girl!* which she did, reading with her skirt clamped between her knees to keep the wind from ripping it off her. The guys draped their jackets over their dates' bare shoulders. But the wind dropped and the sun came out; they made a bonfire on the beach and it was warm enough for kids to dip their toes in the water.

· · · · ·

The music was louder now in the bar, so you could really only hear the person next to you.

"Any kids?" he asked.

"No."

She looked straight ahead, across the room at the backs of the guys sitting at the slot machines.

"We actually. We were trying for quite a while."

"Oh. I'm sorry."

"Yeah, thanks, it's okay. What about you?"

"Me? God, no.... You and Chris should come over for dinner sometime."

· · · · ·

They moved into the gym for the winter. Indoors, everything moved faster. The ball didn't roll away into bushes; there were no breaks to catch your breath while you stood around waiting for someone to go and get it. Here, it bounced off the wall; it was always in play—you ran and ran. At half-time they all sat on the steps leading up to the lobby. She said she wasn't used to the gym.

"I had no idea. I thought, you know, I could really maybe croak. Right here. Heart attack at thirty-four."

"Don't do that."

"I know, right."

"You don't have to chase every ball. Play your position."

"I know."

She jerked her head to one side, flicking her ponytail back over her shoulder, and he remembered that gesture of determination.

"Are you laughing at me?"

"Of course not," he said. "Just ease up on the sprinting."

"It's good exercise."

She smiled directly at him under bangs so straight they could have been measured with a level.

When they were fifteen, they'd filled the sidewalk in that loitering way groups of teenagers have that looks threatening, when really all they want is to be together—a tiny, jostling fortress against uncertainty, adults, embarrassment. They went to someone's house after school, a dozen of them sprawling on plaid furniture, eating crackers and peanut butter. They'd known one another since elementary, some of them since kindergarten. They all believed they'd be best friends for the rest of their lives. He remembered moments like this, looking far into someone's eyes, and then you both laughed until your chest hurt, or you understood them in a way you hadn't before.

· · · · ·

One morning in November he staggered out of bed in a T-shirt and boxers and hugged himself by the window. He shouldered the curtain aside and leaned in to the glass. An icy draft kissed his cheek. All the cars were gone. Instead, a row of white humps, marshmallows lined up on a stick.

The game was cancelled, the street engulfed. The following Wednesday, at work, he caught himself a few times in the act. Of being happy, looking forward, he wasn't even sure to what. To the evening, he thought, the game. He'd missed the exercise.

In the gym, his body felt heavy and slow-moving, his lungs burned, but he got through it. She was improving. He told her so afterwards. She'd tackled him three times and once got the ball away.

"Were you just letting me?"

"You took it fair and square."

She stared up at him belligerently. Her eyes raked over his face like a metal detector, but apparently he came up clean. She stepped back and gave her shoulders a little self-satisfied wriggle.

In the parking lot he popped the trunk and asked if she was going for a drink. She shook her head.

"That bar is disgusting, it smells. And Justin's fine in the gym, but when he opens his mouth he's a jerk."

"Okay. I have beer in the fridge. If you want one."

She flicked her phone on to check the time.

"Ummm, lemme see.... Okay. Sure."

He closed his trunk and then opened it again and tossed his bag in.

On the way home he cast his mind into his living room: what did it look like? If he beat her by thirty seconds he could do a sweep and snatch up anything embarrassing. Not that there was anything embarrassing, probably. But he stepped on the pedal all the same. His house stood near the bottom of a hill; he manoeuvred the car into a parking spot up the road, leaving her the space at the front. The row of clapboard houses looked like a palisade made from posts of different colours. If you drilled a hole the size of a grapefruit behind your TV screen, you could reach into your neighbour's living room and pluck a chip from the bowl on the side table.

He held his front door open as she jogged up the steps and stood back while she came in and undid her boots. She was wearing her gear still, minus the sneakers, a parka over top with fake fur around the hood.

"Jeez, Jess, do you not own a pair of sweatpants?"

Her legs—the bit he could see between the long shorts and high soccer socks—were red with cold.

"It was only to run to the car."

"You're cracked. Have a seat."

He winced as he pushed through the white saloon doors between the living room and the kitchen, which had been there when he bought the house and which he had determined several years ago to take down immediately. Did he think he was living in the fucking Wild West or something? He grabbed bottles from the fridge and an opener from a hook on the wall. She was making her way around the living room, examining a watercolour he'd bought on holiday in Italy.

"It looks like you, here. It looks like a place you would have."

"It's Corona or Quidi Vidi. Or whatever this one is."

"Olé!"

She took the armchair. He set the beer on the coffee table and handed her a blanket from the arm of the couch. Across the road, the Christmas lights always went up the day after Halloween, and now they tossed a string of colours across the picture window. She crossed her legs and cocooned herself in the grey blanket, one limb emerging like a snowman's stick arm to hold her beer bottle.

They talked about the old days, what everyone was up to now—about Ross, in real estate in Toronto doing, so everyone said, a shitload of coke, and although people said it disapprovingly, you could tell some part of them wished they were off in the big city doing a shitload of coke too, just to see what that was like; Trev and Emma and their three children, one of whom had some kind of illness; Martin and Sarah and their sons, who'd moved to Calgary and were just waiting for a transfer home; Holly and Deb and the Christmas party they were throwing to get everyone together, and it was Deborah now, not Deb; Calvin in Switzerland and how he never wanted to set foot here again, but his visa was going to expire— and she politely refused a second beer, disentangled herself from the throw and pulled on her boots.

"Good to see you."

"Thanks for the beer."

· · · · ·

He picked up the empties and took them out to the kitchen. It was good to have old friends. They knew you better than anyone. He opened the fridge to see if there was anything he could pack in a lunch bag in the morning.

He hadn't grown up wanting to be an Estate and Trust Professional, and yet every morning he put on a dark suit and went to a bank near the harbour. He had the right manner for the job. You can't be chatty when people are thinking about death. He asked earnest questions and listened carefully to the answers, making notes on a pad on the right-hand side of his desk. But he wasn't stiff. He paid attention and was ready with a wry comment to relieve an uncomfortable moment. There was no shortage of uncomfortable moments, but he could help to bridge them. He knew about arranging cremations. He'd caused homes to be cleaned and locks to be changed. He understood the difference between a casket and a coffin and could answer questions about what happened to the pension. He'd tracked down beneficiaries from Orlando to Irkutsk.

He made his mortgage payments on time and dressed in layers to keep the heat bill down. He'd thought more about death than other people his age. It wasn't worry, but he had an awareness of the adjustability of timelines. Most of his contemporaries had paired off by now and he wasn't quite sure why he hadn't or whether it was still likely, but he had friends, interests, commitments. He was often out several nights a week. Sometimes he was home just long enough to heat up leftovers.

• • • • •

Jessica came over the next Wednesday after soccer, and the next. They graduated to two beers. At first she'd been reluctant; she didn't want to keep him from the crowd. But he wasn't particularly attached to the crowd. She put her feet up on his coffee table and crossed them, shin guards bulging under the high striped socks. She threw her head back and opened her mouth wide when she laughed. They laughed a lot. He was quick with a joke. He knew he'd succeeded when she slapped her hand a few times on the table or her thigh—it was a kind of applause, a way she had of giving herself over physically to humour, as if she were being swept away by an avalanche of pleasure. Or jumping into the path of one. He couldn't help being swept away too. Making a joke was a kind of puzzle: he would twist something around in his head until it was an idea and then set it off like a firework. Often she groaned or told him how pathetic he was. Then they'd argue.

"Come on, that one was pretty good."

"It sucked."

"It had redeeming qualities."

"Don't kid yourself."

He showed her his basement with its dirt floor and hundred-year-old pony stall. He'd known she'd like that, and the fact that he hadn't taken it out. From his front door, a few feet above the sidewalk, the land sloped away in two directions: downhill to the main road, and away to the small garden at the rear, so at the back of the house, the basement door opened onto a rectangle of grass with a fence at the end and a field behind it. His house had been built across a gap between two others, a gap that had once been a lane-way. The pony had probably pulled a delivery cart.

She stood in front of the stall like someone in a museum, staring intently, as if she could conjure the animal into existence through sheer force of imagination. For a second he could almost see a mane swish in the gloom at the back. He pointed out the faint patches of reddish paint that looked like the remnants of letters in an arc over the stall door, but neither of them could decide what the name had been.

• • • • •

He needed to be a bit careful. He didn't want to give the wrong impression. Didn't want to make a fool of himself. He wasn't a flirter, certainly not with anyone married. They were old friends. He liked her. He liked Darren Fitzpatrick too, who'd also gone to high school with them, and some-times he and Darren played chess and had a couple of beers, and there was nothing unsettling about that.

The second Wednesday in December was the last game before Christmas. The rec centre called in the afternoon. The roads were getting worse and they were closing the building. He'd been busy since lunch and not watching the weather; now he took the long way home to avoid a steep climb from the harbour. The car chugged up to Duckworth on a side street and he gunned it through the stop sign, praying nothing was coming. The wipers flung themselves back and forth in a frenzy, and still he could hardly see the road ahead. He drove east and turned in front of the Hotel. At the red light he realized he'd been hunched forward over the wheel like a jockey and his hip felt weird. And then it didn't. And then it did again. His hip was twitching. His phone was on vibrate. In his pocket.

The light changed and he steered slowly forward with his left hand as he fumbled to undo the buttons of his coat. He knew it was a stupid, dangerous thing to do, he knew whatever it was could wait, and yet he trapped the phone between two fingers. The car slid sideways and his heart lurched—he let go of the phone and grabbed the wheel and drove carefully the rest of the way. As soon as he pulled in front of the house he saw the text. *Want to have a beer anyway?*

She and Chris didn't live far; she could walk. His thumb hovered over the screen for a second but he turned the phone off and jammed it into his pocket. He went inside, turned up the heat, changed out of his suit. He took a shovel and cleared the step of the old lady a few doors up who was afraid of being trapped inside by a drift. Then he did his own steps and the stretch of sidewalk in front of the house. He went back in and brought his phone upstairs. He sat on the bed, towelled his hair dry, typed *OK*.

The plow's flashing orange lights swooped across the closed blind on the front window. There was scraping and the clang of the blade on asphalt and then a thud on the door, which seconds later swung open. She burst in with wind and flakes swirling around her, like a magician.

"Wowsers! It's not that cold, though."

She unwound her scarf and handed it to him, stepping

out of tall green rubber boots. She pushed back her hood and unzipped a down coat, and he took that as well and hung it on a hook at the bottom of the stairs. He was used to seeing her in long shorts and socks and an oversized jersey. She looked more substantial now, more grown-up, in a sweater, a skirt and tights. It was almost disconcerting, but she seemed unchanged otherwise. She followed him through the doorway into the kitchen.

"Didn't you have a door or something there?"

He reached into the fridge, took out two beers and set them on the table.

"I think I have some chips."

He took the chips down from a cupboard and when he turned she was behind him.

"I was reading an article about personal space today. Most people need eight to sixteen inches, but that doesn't seem like very much, does it? I mean, if my face was eight inches from yours, I'm pretty sure you'd think I was in your face."

She tended to defer to him when it came to sports and mathematics. Since she didn't defer much otherwise, this was mildly flattering. He opened his free hand and splayed his fingers to show her: "That's eight and a half inches there."

He held up an index finger to indicate the distance from his face. He was about to take his hand away but she leaned in. Her mouth brushed the tip of his finger.

"I'm done with Chris."

He stood still, taking this in. She looked as solemn as a client. She tipped up her chin. He bent his head to kiss her cheek, which was still cold and tasted of melted snow. He kissed her lips. The inside of her mouth felt friendly. The kitchen seemed like a bright, hard place; he drew her back to the living room. What happened next, if it did happen, would change everything, and if it didn't, that would change everything as well. He held her arm and led her through the doorway. He wondered if he could possibly have misunderstood, and also where the condoms were, if they were all upstairs, and what his bedroom looked like right now. Also he wished he'd had a beer earlier, to feel relaxed. But mostly he wanted his mouth open on hers again, he wanted that now, so when they reached the couch he wrapped his arms loosely around her and kissed her some more, and that was what she seemed to want too. He felt her hands tug at his waist. She pulled his T-shirt and sweater up together and he lifted his arms to wriggle out. She moved her fingers over his chest. She kissed one nipple and then the other and then she raised her mouth back to his.

He liked the sensation of taking a woman in his arms and pulling her to his bare chest, but it wasn't a feeling he wanted to savour indefinitely. He covered her breasts with his hands and felt the stiff, lacy fabric behind the wool. He pulled the sweater over her head and the straps off her shoulders.

They had no ease with each other. Everything was a guess. He reached under her skirt, ran his fingers up her tights until he found the waistband, and pulled down. She took something from the pocket of her skirt. He felt her fingers at the zipper of his jeans, and he undid the button and slid them down. She pushed hard against his chest and he sat back suddenly into the couch. She tossed him a small packet.

He unrolled the condom; she wedged one knee into the couch by his thigh and swung the other over his lap. He ran his fingers under her but she was ready, and he took her hips and angled them. He could feel the soft fabric of her skirt flapping on his knees. Soon he saw her mouth open and felt her clench and clench; she pressed her face into his shoulder. He screwed his eyes shut and braced and heard the sound that was his own breath rushing in.

· · · · ·

The staff room had a view of the harbour, a mini-kitchen, a bulletin board with cards, crayon drawings and notes (*ThANK you for sHoWing US your BanK, LOve Maddie*) and notices about missing pets and 50/50 tickets for charity and how if people didn't wipe out the microwave after use, Chantelle would come after them with a blunt instrument, lol. There were tables and chairs and it wasn't break time yet, so the room was empty. He drank his coffee slowly, looking out the window and then at the phone on the table in front of him, and outside again. It was sunny; two figures in red suits leaned over the side of a Coast Guard icebreaker, using some kind of tool to knock off the icicles. Twice he picked the phone up and put it down. Finally he snatched it off the table and typed a few words, deleted them, and wrote *Hi*. Her answer came within seconds: *Hi*. That was it. He felt a little sick. He watched a huge icicle plunge into the harbour. And then another ping: *You are lovely.*

He could feel the stupid smile spread across his face. He put a hand over his mouth as if he could wipe it off, but it just got bigger. *You too,* he typed. *Busy tonight?* But then he deleted the second bit and replaced it with *Coffee?*

Busy today, she said, *Touch base tomorrow?* So that was that, he thought. But she texted him in the morning: *Going home for lunch?* He waited a moment and said *Yes.* And then: *Coming?* Her reply slid in: *Y.*

He fumbled the key into the deadbolt and felt the little ka-dunk as it turned. He sprinted upstairs, turned on the heat, shook out the duvet, straightened the pillows. He took the stairs two at a time on the way down and stood by the living room window, twisting the wand to close the blind. She was walking just below him, on the other side of the glass, hatless, head down against the snow. He could have reached out and touched the top of her head. It was a vertical blind that had come with the house—broad, nubbled fabric slats that rotated sideways to close the gaps until they stood shoulder to shoulder like soccer players defending a penalty kick and the outside world disappeared. His heart was banging from the stairs. He turned and stepped towards the door as it opened.

"Hey," he said.

She stared at him, her eyebrows raised. It was a moment before she spoke.

"I've never seen you in a suit. Holy. You should wear suits all the time."

His hand went automatically to his tie and he adjusted

it slightly. If she remembered too late that he'd worn a suit at her wedding, she didn't mention it and neither did he. She stood on one leg to pull off her boot; she teetered and his hand shot out to steady her. He'd wondered if he was supposed to offer her lunch, but she stepped off the mat without letting go of his hand and he heard her coat unzipping as she made for the stairs.

His elbows sank into the mattress on either side of her as if it were a snowbank. When he pulled himself up, he saw the print on the wall. It was all green and white: a ship, a storm, an arm of water topped with foam, flinging itself over the heaving bow. When she came he couldn't look down at her; it felt too intimate. Instead he raised his eyes and saw his own face reflected briefly in the glass.

He rolled off, tugged the duvet up over her shoulders, and lay on his back. He would call in sick for the afternoon. There was no need to go anywhere. Maybe another blizzard would hit. She could be stranded here. He would forage for food in the kitchen and bring it back, he would feed her in bed, they would stay here for days. He felt her lips on his cheek and opened his eyes. He wondered if he was satisfactory. He wanted to be told he was doing a good job.

"I have to go," she whispered.

It was the first thing either of them had said since she arrived.

· · · · ·

He wasn't going to Holly and Deborah's Christmas party. Saturday was his mother's birthday and there would be a family dinner at Tammy's. Tammy and Wayne lived well beyond the overpass, so by the time he got back it wouldn't be worth it. And then his dad's cough turned into bronchitis. His mom said they weren't setting foot out the door until the antibiotics kicked in. He stopped over and gave his mom a poinsettia and a gift certificate.

"How's he sleeping?"

"It's like lying there listening to the filter on an aquarium all night. I feel like a tropical fish. Glug."

She waved her hands at her sides in a way that was supposed to suggest fins.

He sat with his dad a while, and an hour later he was perched on a barstool in Holly and Deborah's recently renovated kitchen with a beer, catching up with Ross, who was home for Christmas and showing no obvious signs of a major coke habit. It was all matching steel appliances and sleek pendant lamps and stone countertops. He didn't usually pay attention to how anyone had anything decorated, but looking around the room made him realize that his kitchen looked like other people's did twenty years ago.

The noise level had risen since he'd arrived, boots spewing like lava from the porch into the hall, someone's kid plunking out "Jingle Bells" on the piano in the next room over a playlist of '90s hits. He felt the draft at his back that meant someone else had arrived.

"Heya!" Ross said.

He turned and saw Chris. There was no point pretending: he'd never liked Chris, who was an arrogant prick, and now he wanted to stand and smash him in the face. Chris had his arm around a woman in a sparkly black dress and heels. Jessica.

The mouthful of beer hung at the back of his throat, suspended like a tree ornament and threatening to rise back up. He felt strange. He thought he might fall off the stool. He didn't make eye contact with her as he stood.

"Hey man," he said to Chris.

He got out as soon as he could. At home, he let his phone judder and buzz on the kitchen table and lay in bed wide awake with rage for a long time.

Surely there are limits to what you can be expected to do as a decent human being. Surely if someone says *I'm done with insert-husband's-name-here*, you are not morally obliged to produce a three-page questionnaire, to demand a precise definition of *done* or to verify that insert-husband's-name-here's understanding of the situation corresponds fairly closely to that of your interlocutor. *I'm done* communicates a certain operational understanding, a working knowledge. It says Don't worry, you may proceed.

· · · · ·

Late Sunday morning he was stretched out on the couch watching the Premier League. He'd picked up a coffee and a bagel at the new place around the corner, and he was thinking he should call his dad in a bit and then maybe buy groceries. There was knocking and the door opened. She stepped inside, leaning back to close it.

"You don't have to assume I'm a bitch, you know. It wouldn't have killed you to answer your phone."

He was enjoying his anger. He gave himself over to its energy. It carried a thrill—unlike disappointment or shame or any of the other things you feel when you've been screwed over. He watched her without interest and heard the uncertainty in her voice, which was satisfying.

"So. Can I come in?"

"Whatever."

He turned back to the game and picked up his coffee, but she crossed the room and stood in front of the screen. Her face was pale and blotchy. The wind had yanked some hair out of her ponytail, flicking it over her face.

"You think I lied to you and I didn't. We did decide to split up. I stayed with my cousin for a few days. He wanted to try again, he wanted me to go to the party. I thought you weren't going."

She stood awkwardly, looking down at him, hands thrust into the pockets of her black down coat, the toe of one striped sock lapped over the other. He waited. His voice felt tight and quiet when he spoke.

"Is that the absolute truth? The honest-to-god truth? Don't mess with me, Jess."

They locked eyes.

"On Wednesday night we were officially not a couple. I swear to god."

He left her standing there for a while and then pulled his legs off the couch and sat up to make room for her, but she didn't move.

"Are you still split up? Wait a second. What about Friday, at lunchtime?"

She didn't answer.

"Fucksake."

"He had an affair. With someone at work. He wants to stay together, but."

"So...I'm revenge. I'm helping you balance things out? Jesus."

He felt no compassion. Or he tried to push it away. She looked miserable. She felt betrayed, he knew this, by her shit of a husband—and he had been betrayed as well.

Not betrayed. Used. But probably she hadn't set out to use him.

"I know what you're thinking, but Chris isn't really.... It was a tough time. We were trying to have kids. It's all about sex, but there's nothing sexy about it. You're just a machine. A machine that doesn't work."

She sat down at the other end of the couch and looked straight ahead at the TV. The player ran towards the ball to take a penalty kick. As his foot made contact, she dropped her eyes to the floor.

"It was Chris. Why we couldn't have kids. It was hard news for him to take on. He wanted to feel sexy with someone, I guess. Yes, I want him chopped up in freezer bags. But I felt that way too."

She turned towards him.

"It wasn't revenge. I wouldn't do that. I love coming here, after soccer."

He heard her voice wobble but she recovered. She stared at him, fierce with effort. As if he'd done something wrong.

"I wanted to be with you. I think about you all the time. I imagine you at work. In your suit."

She said this as if it were something he had done to her against her will, as if he'd forced the thought of his suit into her head. He thought about her imagining him at work, whatever that meant, and then he was shifting his position and sitting up straighter and wishing she would take her coat off.

"I think"—he said it reasonably gently—"I think you'd better go."

He'd never thought of himself as someone who would sleep with another man's wife. He wasn't that kind of guy.

At work on Monday he was distracted by long, twisty streams of thought that he kept needing to follow through to their conclusion. Two sisters had been arguing over their mother's estate. The sister he didn't like sat in his office. Attractive, narrow skirt, crossed legs. She had a chain with a shiny green stone around her neck; the stone hung in an elegant cage of silver. He was trying hard to pay attention, but he thought the necklace would look good on Jess, and then he was thinking about cabins, a cabin in the woods.

If you were out hiking on a nice day and you decided to get comfortable and you beat the padlock off the door and used the stuff in the cabin and left, you'd be an asshole. But if you were caught in a blizzard out there, you'd find something to bust that padlock off and you'd shelter and make a fire so you didn't freeze to death, and the next day when things had settled down, you'd tidy up and leave a note and maybe you'd go back another time and leave some wood and a bottle of rum. And there was absolutely nothing wrong with that. When you had your shoulder to the cabin door you wouldn't think twice about it because getting in would be everything that mattered. And once or twice, just briefly, he'd thought maybe what mattered more than most things was Jess pulling him on top of her, feeling her body move under his, the ship above them pushing steadily on though the storm.

He wasn't a cabin connoisseur; his family hadn't gone in for cabins. And the cabin was obviously not the best parallel. The point was contingency. The same situation, and only the circumstances made it right or wrong.

Somehow, the attractive, obnoxious sister was still talking.

"And every time it's how much she did for Mom, well, no one was holding a gun to her head. I can't be flying home every weekend."

"Yes."

He was thinking of his bed, Jess pressing her face into him and making a small noise. He wanted to put his arms around her, to protect her from something. From anything. Or for her to protect him.

"Yes what?"

The long-legged sister was scowling.

"Yes, I understand, it's been.... It's been difficult."

Maybe he'd caught his dad's bronchitis. He felt dazed, muzzy. It was dark when he left work. At home he left his coat on and stood in the middle of the kitchen. The floor felt cold and hard under his socks and he was going to text her. He didn't give a shit about Chris anymore or whether they were married or divorced or had turned into aardvarks. He'd acted in good faith and now here he was, standing on icy linoleum, unable to decide whether to sit down.

He couldn't say anything cavalier or jokey or non-committal. He had nothing left. He thought about saying *I have pneumonia.* Maybe she'd come to look after him.

He typed, *Where are you?*

Outside.

Thanks be to Christ. He strode to the front door and flung it open. He heard a car door slam and then he was stepping aside to let her in.

· · · · ·

He woke in the night feeling warm. He pushed the duvet aside and started when his hand touched her shoulder.

She would leave in the morning and it would be over. Or he'd bring her coffee in bed and, later, cook some eggs, and in five years, ten years, he would still be bringing her coffee in bed. Chris would disappear, or not, or eventually make her pregnant, or not. He couldn't control that. She was lying on her side and he tucked his thighs under hers. Her back felt warm against his chest. He angled himself around her body like the corner of a fitted sheet.

He hadn't drawn the bedroom curtain. He could see the streetlight across the road. A pattern of snowflakes swished violently left and right in front of it like a square of lace in a hurricane. In an hour he'd be able to stand on his own front steps and not recognize the houses across the way—ice pellets driving into his face, everything a shifting mass of white.

THE DINNER

CATHY SAW FROM her kitchen window a car pulling into the driveway below. She watched the passenger door yawn open. A clear plastic cake dome appeared first, and then Pam's black boot below a sturdy calf, and then another boot, and then the rest of Pam, long limbs and chestnut hair, a bag hanging from her shoulder, wrapping herself around the dome the way the centre arches his body over the football before the snap.

Cathy cranked the window, which yanked away from its seal with a sound like a slow, smacking kiss. She felt the lick of cool air on her cheek and heard Pam's voice wafting up.

"Thanks, honey," Pam was saying. "I'll get a cab home." With a twist of her hip, she swung the car door shut. Pam seemed to be looking past the car and out at something, so Cathy looked too, and there was Angela, hopping towards them like a robin along the icy sidewalk. She had a backpack and red scarf, black curls spilling down over her shoulders. Angela waved and Pam, still holding the cake dome, nodded extravagantly to make up for not waving. Cathy didn't want to call out and startle Pam into dropping the cake.

It had begun. They were converging, the three of them, on this split-level with grey vinyl siding in the northeast end because they were a hundred and fifty now, collectively. Pam was the last of them to hit the half-century point—her birthday had been two days earlier. It was a marker, the beginning of a second half, or possibly a final third, or, well, maybe not that much, but a marker worthy of attention in any case.

Cathy herself had not converged, of course: she lived there. And Angela hadn't quite converged yet, but almost. Several times her feet had nearly shot out in front of her and she'd thought she would fall backwards, onto the bottles of wine in her knapsack, and there would be blood and chunks of glass and possibly a broken bone or two, but despite those thoughts, Angela was enjoying herself already, without even having arrived yet: the anticipation, the getting away from the house, leaving them to sort themselves out for a while—she was escaping and the evening air smelled clean and there would be who knows what. There would certainly be food and drink and much talk and laughing, but it was more than that, their own triple-fiftieth birthday during their country's hundred and fiftieth, which surely meant something. They would make it epic. She saw Pam in the driveway waiting for her, and the two of them proceeded carefully along the path so as not to fling themselves, the wine, and the cake into a mangled heap, but Cathy had shovelled and salted, and whatever disasters awaited them in the next stage of life, slipping on this path would not be one of them.

They stood at the front door, hesitating, tiny salt chunks crunching underfoot. Pam nudged Angela, who looked at her and rolled her eyes just a little, and they waited there for a moment. Then Angela pressed the bell, turned the handle, and pushed the door open.

The wooden floor gleamed; they could smell herbs and wine, maybe chicken. Cathy appeared in the hallway in capri leggings and a turquoise tunic, reaching for their coats. Her hair was done in a neat blonde bob; a jagged cluster of silver hung below her neck, and she had something stuck to her leg, Pam noticed, a shiny piece of plastic wrap. It looked deliberate and Cathy hadn't said anything about a medical procedure, so Pam didn't ask. Yet.

They flopped into the sage green suede-ish loveseat and armchairs in the living room. Cathy had laid a tray on the coffee table, and now pale yellow fizz was running into the flutes she'd set out, alongside vegetables and dip, olives, and some twirly cheese pastries.

Whatever happens, Cathy thought, I'm not going to tell them about Morgan. There's no need.

Angela curled up in the corner of the loveseat, lifting a hip to slide a phone from her pocket. She set it on the armrest.

"Everything okay on the home front?" Pam asked.

"Oh yes," Angela said, "thanks." Angela wasn't going to hijack the evening with tales of woe. She smiled.

Angela was beautiful. She'd always been beautiful, but when they were children they hadn't noticed. She had curly black hair that gleamed and skin that was dark enough that it never looked pale or blemished or otherwise uneven; she had worn, for as long as Cathy or Pam could remember—or nearly that long—shiny deep red lipstick that matched the colour of her cheeks when she blushed.

Everything was not okay on the home front, but it was better than it had been. Angela had called Pam from outside the emergency room once, hysterical. Pam was in her government office in the Confederation Building, a command-and-control centre where she sat behind a desk sending messages and making calls, performing banal-looking actions that mobilized logistical support in the service of an astonishing variety of complex operations. Pam was a kind of government giant squid, a highly intelligent cephalopod operating well below the surface, agile and with tentacles capable of spectacular silent reach. She could hear the sound on the cellphone moving in and out as Angela paced; she was crying and could barely get the words out, and it was a while before Pam understood what she wanted: Angela was supposed to give a paper; the doctor had said Angela should stay with Benjamin until he saw the specialist, who might arrive at any moment or in five or seven hours, and Angela wanted Michael to come and take her place just for a bit, but the doctor felt she should stay, because the specialist would probably decide whether to admit Benjamin to hospital or not, and if there was an admission it would probably not be overnight; it would be a lengthy admission, and Angela should be there for that discussion. Angela had been at the hospital for hours already and she'd been asked to give the paper eight months earlier. "You want me to call them and cancel for you?" said Pam. In fact Angela wasn't sure what she wanted; she had called Pam because Pam was calm and knew how to make things happen, all sorts of things—if someone had to be located, Pam knew the first three places to try, and the next four, and all the places after that. "You want someone to give the paper for you, is that it?" Pam had said, without much to base this on, and it turned out that was exactly what Angela did want. "I'll see if Cathy can do it: you email me the paper now and I'll call you back in a few minutes, okay? Don't worry, we're on it."

"Thank you," Angela whispered, and then she was gone and back inside the hospital. Pam called Cathy's secretary, who slipped into a meeting with a note, and Cathy stepped out to take the call.

"She wants me to *give* the paper?" Cathy said.

"It's already written, you just have to read it out, it's about the viability of alternatives to traditional methods of fish farming—"

"Christ," said Cathy. "Okay, can you send it now? I'll be free in about ten minutes; I'll look it over."

"It's in your inbox," Pam said, and she knew Cathy's quick mind would shoot through that paper in the taxi, sending out search beams to detect anything that might make her stumble, and smooth it out, and within an hour she'd stride to the front of the room in her suit, past all the marine biologists in their flannel and khaki, she'd set the paper on the lectern and look out at the room and feel for the chain that held her reading glasses and position them on her nose, and no one would question her authority.

Unavoidably detained, she'd said, and then it was aquaculture and sea lice and tanks, statistics and on-land options and how best to decrease rates of antibiotic use, and she was so convincing several hands went up at the end.

"No questions. Please follow up with Dr. Marshall if there's something urgent—" and Cathy sailed out of there, for all the world like the executive scientist they thought she must be.

Cathy wore suits a lot for work, not just when she had to address a gathering; she managed lots of people at the kind of place you were expected to wear suits, only some people fared better in suits than others. Cathy liked to say that her height-weight ratio wasn't optimal. Half the time she felt as if she'd been wrestled and stuffed into one of her grey or navy ensembles; when she caught sight of herself in the mirror, she thought she looked like an egg in an egg cozy. Her grandmother used to have egg cozies; Cathy had grown up in Nan's little row house and had toast from the toast rack and the green knitted cozy on her egg. When you opened Nan's front door and took three steps down, you were already on the sidewalk, which was on a hill, and sometimes in winter you could slide down the whole street on a sled, as long as Nan was standing at the bottom in her black ankle boots with the fur around the top, to make sure you didn't shoot out onto the busier road at the bottom. Nan didn't like the winter anymore, she was always worrying about the power going out and being snowed in, she was afraid of drifts and not being able to open the door and being trapped in the house if there was a fire, but luckily there was a nice young man a few doors down— Nan always called him that, the Nice Young Man—who came and shovelled her out, and Cathy had never actually laid eyes on the Nice Young Man but she kept meaning to seek him out, to go over with a bottle of brandy or something, to thank him for keeping an eye; he must know how Nan felt about the drifts and the door because she'd told Cathy he often shovelled around her door before he did his own. Cathy would go over soon and tell him how much she appreciated him. She'd even bought a fancy bottle and stashed it away, she'd had it for a month or more, waiting to get around to it. In fact, she had begun to feel queasy at not having delivered that bottle: she saw it as negligence and feared punishment. She tried not to think about it sitting in the front hall closet like a reminder of her many failings. Sometime in the next few years her nan would die, and that was one of the things Cathy thought about when she lay awake at 3:37 a.m.: how, although Nan was ninety-one and getting frailer and sometimes unreasonable, she had been pouring her love unstoppably into Cathy for fifty years and that was a pretty goddam powerful thing and it had shaped her. Cathy had a hard time thinking about getting up in the morning and knowing that Nan was not over in her house making a cup of tea or doing a bit of dusting or listening to the radio or whatever the hell she did all day. Cathy did not want the world not to have her nan in it and she worried about her having a fall and lying alone until she was found, and she worried about Morgan, her holier-than-thou vegan daughter who wasn't quite so holier-than-thou since Cathy had seen her smoking downtown outside the restaurant where she waited tables; Cathy had been hand-delivering some extremely confidential documents in the middle of the afternoon when she walked right past the pee-smelling alley that ran along the side of the restaurant. It wasn't until she was in front of the display of shoes in the next building that it hit her—the angle of the hips, the slant of the neck—and she hadn't turned back because she'd been biding her time, you had to pick your battles, she'd been playing that one carefully, but Morgan had seen her, had seen her seeing, and there had been a lot less said about Cathy's irresponsible dietary habits after that.

And now the smoking seemed minor, she could easily shut up about the smoking, if it meant Morgan would be close and safe and speaking to her.

The three of them started with the catching-up talk, the latest news, the family updates, the miscellaneous gossip, all of which was fine and enjoyable and which needed to be got through before they could get into the serious business of the evening, the stories, the cackles and guffaws, the revelations, the remembering, the gradual laying bare of the soul, the moments of offering up your worst fears to the people you'd trust with your life and having them explain what an idiot you are or watching them take on your fear as their own and acknowledge its weight and still manage to have you laughing a few minutes later. They would cover a table with their problems as if they were in a tapas bar, and each one would be scrutinized, and suggestions would be proffered: what needed to be added or taken away, what might be tried, who must be spoken to. And they would each leave feeling that the hopeless thing was not hopeless after all: it was a question of a different approach, a new strategy; there was a plan. They dealt in hope, in camaraderie, in forgiveness, in assuming the others' best intentions and being prepared to overlook minor lapses, which was what they had always done. But for now they were picking at the olives and pouring more bubbly and skating over the surface of their lives: Michael's promotion and Pam's new boss and the bitchy, paranoid girlfriend of Cathy's ex, Don.

Pam almost never drank sparkling wine—it rarely occurred to her to celebrate things, although it seemed, increasingly, a good idea—and she was loving this one, how it felt excitable and prickly and teasing in her mouth. She'd bought a nice Italian something or other to bring this evening, and the guy who rang her in was barely older than her Luke, one of those young men who seemed to have their hair upside down, a shaved head although he was too young to be bald, and an absurdly long beard, as if all his hair had grown the wrong way somehow. And yet in spite of that she loved him. Many of Pam's feelings these days were almost overpowering; she knew it was biochemical, hormonal, temporary, but what she experienced didn't seem like the swing of a chemical sledgehammer; it seemed suffused with warmth, affection, undertone and nuance. She loved this liquor store man, she felt, in an almost metaphysical way, a way that respected his qualities, his abilities (whatever they might be), and had nothing (or at least not very much) to do with the fact that she could imagine the store closed, the lights off, lying back on the counter by the cash with his liquor store shirt folded up behind her head where he chivalrously had placed it—it wasn't just lust, because she was awfully fond of him already, and she sensed that he knew that and that he felt the same way. Rod would stride out of the bathroom in the morning, his penis flapping from one side to the other with every step he took, as if it were trying to decide something—eeny meeny miney mo—and she'd think, Pick me! Pick me! and he'd reach for a pair of clean coveralls and say We're blocked with bodywork again all week, it's the black ice, I might grab a bite of supper at work with Barry, see if we can get ahead of it.

It must be admitted that Pam did have a bit of a thing for men taking off their shirts—any shirts, not just liquor store ones—or not bothering to put them on to begin with; shirtless men popped into her head for no good reason, at all hours of the day and night, guys pulling off T-shirts all the better to reach an itch and then clean forgetting to slip back into them; loosening a tie and a top button and then distractedly carrying on to the next button and the next, as if they'd just accidentally wandered off course from what they'd set out to do. Muscle definition? She couldn't care less.

A little softness, a friendly paunch, a tiny scrubby patch of hair sitting over the sternum or a shag carpet of something that looked like it had been ripped off the hindquarters of a muskox: it was all good, and despite her resistance, her attempts to distract herself, despite everything she knew to be correct and appropriate, of all those men parading through her mind, the one who kept coming back was Glenn.

"C'mon, Pammie." Angela was standing and gesturing towards the dining room. "Your meal awaits." Cathy was already in there, in the dark; Pam saw her take a box from the mantel, strike a match, and hold it up. The flame burst and wiggled and then held steady, Cathy's face a warm yellow as if she were part of a Caravaggio tableau, guiding them through the darkness; she leaned over and lit a circle of tea lights at the centre of the table, and then she reached for a dimmer switch on the wall and adjusted it. "The salad is on the counter, Ange, the blue bowl. And Pam, that wine you brought is out there too, please."

Angela loved the candles, the low, warm light, the feeling of intimacy; she had spent too much time in over-lit institutional rooms lately and she wished this evening would extend indefinitely—Angela had done her best, most of the time, to keep it together, to maintain some semblance of dignity, but now and then it got the better of her. She'd spent nights on a yoga mat on the hardwood floor in the hall outside Benjamin's room so she'd know if he was up— just in case. And now, despite her earlier determination, she found herself launching into a tale of woe, and not even a recent one; she was reliving with them a day in the fall when she'd been stuck in the hospital elevator, what kind of luck was that, locked in with Benjamin and a nurse for half an hour between floors—and when they finally made it out she had, humiliatingly, wept in front of some officious woman with a clipboard asking more questions. She had wept in the lineup to register at Emergency on New Year's Day, when she couldn't bear it that they were back there again, that it wasn't getting better (weren't things supposed to get better?), there was a painted red line on the floor you weren't supposed to cross so you wouldn't hear the person in front of you registering at the Plexigas window, which you heard anyway, and Angela hadn't had a tissue and she was so tired, she hadn't really slept in months and she could sense that she was losing her grip sometimes, because she didn't seem to be able to think anymore, she didn't actually have thoughts; thoughts would flit limply around in her vicinity instead of developing in her head, and she'd have to try to snag one as it passed and examine it to see if it was useful; her stomach had been hurting forever, it hurt all the time, it felt like one of those Second World War sea mines, round and black and hard, with spiky things sticking out of it, she had really hoped not to be standing in that line again and she didn't have a tissue and stuff was running out of her nose; she'd read the websites and the books and the online forums, she'd used every strategy she knew and nothing had worked, sometimes it made it worse. There were no ideas left. Benjamin was not reachable, or only occasionally. She'd sniffed and dug around in her clothes for any old bit of wadded-up tissue and finally found a soft dry thing, and just feeling it there offered some relief, so when she pulled it out of the back pocket of her trousers and saw it was a tea bag, she stared at it in disbelief verging on despair.

"A tea bag."

"I don't know, Cath, I don't know what it was doing there."

When the doctor had spoken in the examining room that day in the fall, Angela had been afraid—the nice doctor, they'd seen her lots of times, but this time her face was grim and set and it was dawning on Angela that she could fight all she wanted, she could throw everything at this; she could grab Ben and claw her way along, pulling him with her through the sheer force of her body and her will, but when she saw the doctor's determined face, she realized finally that it might not be enough; this might not be a battle she could win, because it wasn't her battle. And if she failed, what she forfeited could be the life of her son.

"No Ange, later is not good enough. We are all fifty now and as a result we're going to have to get polluted here tonight." Cathy moved Angela's hand off the top of her glass and refilled it. "Sometimes you have to go off duty."

"You need to keep your end up," Pam said. "You won't have to do it again until you're a hundred if you don't want to. It'll be okay." And Angela gave in; she felt relaxed and safe and nothing bad was happening; she was going to trust and let go.

"Now just to be clear," Cathy explained, "we are NOT—" she was trying to spear a slim rectangle of red pepper on her fork, but the red pepper had been roasted and then rinsed in lemon mustard dressing, and Cathy's fork chased it around the plate, plunging occasionally, the red pepper always one slippery sideways wriggle away, but now, after a period of deceptive stillness, the tines bore down suddenly, a triple piercing, and Cathy brandished it like a little red flag as she spoke "—NOT going to sit here and talk about fucking MENO-pause." The flag waved briefly and disappeared between Cathy's parted lips, which closed as she stared first at Pam and then at Angela, daring them to challenge her. And then, since no one had challenged her and this was perhaps after all disappointing, she tried again: "We are NOT going to sit around complaining about our bodies like a bunch of old women."

"But that's what we are," Angela said. They had reached an age when the world begins to see women as invisible, ineffectual, post-sexual, when women are frantically dyeing their hair—only you don't call it *dye*, you call it *colour*, which sounds nicer, no suggestion of the tomb in *colour*—they dye their hair because it would otherwise be grey, and grey is increasingly the direction in which they are headed: grey hair, grey skin, a grey stone with a pithy epitaph, and to push against that stone they rush into stores and buy up shelves of dye, cramming it into baskets, all shades and tints, some of it ammonia-free so you don't wreck your kidneys, or is it your brain, all to avoid the ultimate evening-out, the evening, the removal of all colour; already they were on the road to being interchangeable, which was why Angela's Michael could never tell women apart on his walk around the lake—I saw

Suzanne Parker, he'd said, I was pretty sure it was Suzanne but there were three of her on the path—and when Angela reminded him that Suzanne was in Qatar working to keep Emily in law school after that dick left her, he said maybe it wasn't Suzanne after all but it wasn't his fault they all looked alike, these women with their shortish grey hair and their friendly greetings and their sturdy, outdoorsy footwear.

Pam wouldn't have minded talking about menopause. She'd have appreciated some input. She knew the power of hormones in flux. The irony for Pam was that she was becoming acutely aware of her own sexuality just as the entire world was coming to overlook it completely. And, as often happened when her mind wandered this way, it turned to Glenn. She and Rod had been friends with Glenn and his wife, Trisha, forever, so of course nothing would happen. And Glenn would be horrified to learn that she had any thoughts like that at all. No doubt. But Glenn had worn well; he was one of those guys who'd been geeky in school and parlayed what was at the time an unfashionable intelligence into a high-paying job with a medical tech firm. He and Trisha travelled a lot. When they came over for a barbecue or the four of them went for a weekend out of town together, he wore tailored Italian shirts with little dark flowers. Because it is absolutely not okay to have inappropriate thoughts about a close friend, Pam did not entertain any. Until a year or two ago, when she decided that what stayed locked up inside her head wasn't going to do anyone any harm. She felt confident Glenn wasn't interested in her. She noticed small things he did for Trisha, holding a cardigan out for her to put on instead of just handing it over. Slipping an arm around her. She couldn't remember when Rod might have put an arm around her; if he did, it was decades ago. Glenn had an easy manliness of manner that was solar systems away from his youth on Planet Dork. It wasn't clear how he had acquired social skills, but he wielded them now unconsciously and to noticeable effect. Even the glasses he'd hated in school worked to his advantage—not the same ones, of course, but Pam had seen him pull on his half-frames to examine a menu; she had watched the waitress take in the intellectual air, the silver in his sideburns.

The window was black except for the reflection of the three of them at the table, with its circle of candles. Pam sat facing the window and Angela watched her image in it, Pam's square, strong shoulders that had borne the weight of everyone's world at one time or another, Pam who had been calm and sensible and sat people down at her own table and plugged in the kettle and listened and sorted them out or hopped in the car to do the necessary, Pam who had kept track and been reliable and issued reminders and fed and watered, and who might, Angela sensed, be starting to feel that she was ready to retire from taking care of everyone's shit, whose gently rounded cheeks were now glowing pink, brown hair waving gently down to a soft curl at the base of her neck. Pam was listening to Cathy, paying attention, with a finger on her lips and a frown, and then Cathy said something funny and Pam's face unfolded into a smile that burst out from the inside, her face as full of life as the pomegranate seeds glistening in the salad.

They were finishing that salad and using the rolls to wipe the dressing from their plates. Cathy had hesitated over the butter.

"I went out for lunch yesterday," she said. "I used up some of my points...." Morgan's departure was large and frightening, so Cathy spooned that worry out onto other things—managing a difficult staff member, tracking her points. Diffusing the bad thing meant it was everywhere, but in smaller quantities that you might be able to overlook.

"Oh no." Pam spoke with great firmness. "We are not going to a talk about what we ate yesterday. Unless it was fabulous. Yesterday is over, and today we are having butter. In fact, we are never going to regret what we ate yesterday. We're not going to regret anything ever again." She lifted her glass and held it up until they raised theirs and clinked, and thus regret was banished.

They'd been friends since the time of the pterodactyls, the time of white blouses and black pleated tunics. It was Angela who'd found the other two by Cathy's locker and told them John Lennon had been shot. They hadn't believed her at first, and then they'd all cried: their last year of junior high and already the side of light had lost. They'd sat in high school classrooms where teachers kept the radio on after the *Ocean Ranger* went down, and as the names were read out, some students had stood quietly and packed up their books and left. They had watched Lady Di become a princess in her magic puffy dress and gone to bed sixteen years later fully convinced that the morning news would include accounts of a lengthy and successful intervention by French surgeons. They'd come home from university and seen television replays where the announcer falls silent as the *Challenger* writhes in the air, tracing thick, furry white lines through the sky that make shapes like balloon art: a duck, a snail's head, an octopus. And then Chernobyl, where food still sits on plates, on tables, in kitchens abandoned between one mouthful and the next. They'd wanted to go to Berlin when the wall came down but couldn't afford the airfare. They'd watched plywood go up over one store window after another as the cod moratorium dragged on. Angela had actually been there for the announcement: not long out of grad school, looking for a job in her field, she'd had part-time work at the Hotel and had stood in her uniform with her back against the wall in the ballroom with Minister Crosbie, in case anyone signalled for a fresh jug of water; she'd heard the heavy rhythmic banging on the door while the security guard spoke urgently into his walkie-talkie—some men rammed the legs of a chair through the bars of the door to jam it closed, and the worst thing had been not knowing what was happening on the other side, what would happen if the doors burst open, what would come in. Pam was in labour when Timothy McVeigh set off an explosion at the Alfred P. Murrah Federal Building in Oklahoma City, detonating explosives in a truck he'd parked in a drop-off zone under the daycare. Her memory of the days following Luke's birth consisted of a mixture of images: her breasts like enormous concrete bottles of the milk she tried, excruciatingly, to have the baby suck while the television ran photos of a young man in orange coveralls who had taken it into his head that blowing up toddlers was a good idea. There had been Rwanda, there'd been Iraq. Indonesia had been laid low by a giant wave, and later came Japan's turn, the reactor leaking toxic crap all over the place and everything overheating alarmingly, radio-actively, but what had stayed with Cathy was a short clip of that wave travelling rapidly towards the right of the frame—devouring buildings, crops, cars—and a man riding a bicycle ahead of it, on a road between two fields. He was riding as fast as he could, but the wave kept gaining ground.

Cathy, who had forbidden all talk of menopause, was the one going on about it now, about the lack of it. "I can smell it," she said, "stale blood, when I wake up in the night, it's disgusting, there's no need for my fecundity to keep churning on like this, my *youngest* is sixteen for god's sake, I'm done with that, no wonder I can't get my iron levels up, I'm like one of those toads, or is it frogs, those ones that spray a secret poison at their enemies—" ("They're beetles," interjected Angela, the biologist) "—beetles, then, they're beetles and they spew some kind of toxic spray from their bums—yes, exactly, well this might not be toxic but it stains everything, I'm washing the sheets all the time, sleeping on a towel and twisting in front of the mirror to see if I'm fit to be in public and I'm FUCKING sick of it." What Cathy did-n't say as all this gushed out of her was how she felt, lying there alone at three o'clock in the morning, the time when every bad thing swelled darkly from the shadows to fill the whole room, sucked the air out of it and pressed her down into the bed as she struggled to force her muscles to let go—relax your shoulders, relax your jaw, relax and sleep will come, let go of the goddam jaw—smelling blood, the smell of death.

Angela pushed back her chair, collected the salad plates, and brought them to the kitchen, where Cathy was now taking a bowl of green beans from the oven. Angela followed her to the table with the rice, Pam bringing up the rear with the chicken stew, like three kings bearing their gifts.

"Yes," Cathy was saying, "I'm fucking fat, this is not news—no, Pam, this isn't regret, it's about change, just listen, I'm all over it, I have a personal trainer now, oh yes, he's about eleven and he's called Brad, they're all about eleven, it turns out, and they're all called Brad, and I did fricking fartees or whatever they are, the other day, what a nightmare. I hate that place, that gym, all those people with their ridiculous leggings and their overpriced water bottles, what's wrong with them, that they need to be carrying around humongous water bottles all the time—do they leak, those people? This whole water thing is bullshit. Can you remember *any*one having a water bottle when we were growing up? Ever?" She glared at them.

Pam was studying Cathy incredulously. Pam had played competitive volleyball and less competitive basketball and had swum creditably; Pam was obviously not in her athletic prime at this point, having been softened by the three boys and Olivia and years spent making food, providing food, being with food, many times a day, by a fondness for cookies, but she still knew a thing or two about exercise.

Pam said, "Do you mean *burpees*?"

"Sure, burpees, whatever. And lunges and god knows what. I'm not giving in to it," Cathy said. "Age. I'm not going there. I had a tattoo this afternoon, look." She reached down and flicked her shoes off with a finger, grasped the back of her chair, and with one wobble jumped up on the seat.

"Holy cow, look at you! Come on, get that up on the table where we can see it." Angela dragged the beans aside to make space and held out a hand. Cathy grabbed it and set one foot carefully on the round walnut tabletop. She'd had a pedi with hot pink polish. "I'm supposed to take that off now anyway." She tugged at the edge of the plastic wrap above her ankle and off it came, revealing a hand clasping the hilt of a sword. Cathy's feet were small and dainty; she lifted her heel, twisting it in one direction and then the other.

"Catharama!" Angela was leaning over the table for a better look. The sword pointed upward in triumph and slightly to the side, as if sniffing out the next target. The hand clasped the hilt within a protective basket of ornate woven metal. "Look at the detail!"

"That's the attitude I want for the next fifty," Cathy said. "Brandishing, not being slain." She was committed to brandishing, determined to slash left and right and then keep thrusting forward until the dark shadows of the night retreated, until whatever was unsettling Morgan turned tail and ran; she wanted to stand guard over her nan, blade glinting in the darkness.

"How much did it hurt?" Pam said. "I want one. Let's all brandish." She passed Cathy up her glass and Cathy, still pushing and pulling on Angela's hand to stay balanced, raised it towards the ceiling. Pam and Angela lifted their glasses and instead of drinking, the three of them stood like that for a moment around the table, arms raised at the ready. And then Cathy tipped her glass up quickly, swallowed, whipped her hot pink toenails down onto the chair and then under the table and slipped them back in her shoes.

The plastic film over Cathy's tattoo made Angela think of hospitals. She checked her phone to make sure it was on and the volume was maxed. Michael was at home anyway. He and Benjamin and Rebecca all knew where she was, just in case they needed anything, which they wouldn't, because things had settled down a lot lately. Angela imagined herself as someone in one of those Evolution of Man posters, where Man starts out all bent over and simian-looking and ends up proud and erect and spear-carrying. Except that she'd started out standing up with the spear and gone into reverse, and had only lately been crawling her way back up the developmental ladder. Initially it had all seemed quite hopeful: there would probably be a cause and a corresponding treatment. There had been dozens of appointments in which professionals raked through the family history for the one clue that would point them in the direction of an explanation: was there this, did anyone have that, had anyone ever, what about her parents—Lebanon, really? Had there been any traumatic events? Babysitters, friends and influences, the tests, the bloodwork...and slowly she'd learned that there was no answer. Or there were many answers, none of which quite fit. Lots of families, they'd been told, did not do well with these kinds of pressures. Couples sniped and snapped; they hardened like statues and broke into rubble. Counselling was strongly recommended. But, for no reason Angela knew, she and Michael did not do those things. They had never disagreed about how to be parents, and now they hung onto each other out of necessity, but also out of desire. Michael was still a good-looking man: tall and square, with short hair, dark eyes, and a general air of deep, smoky quiet. The previous night she'd got up because she'd heard a noise, but it had been the people across the road coming home from a party. She had returned and stood by the bed watching him for a moment. She'd leaned over and kissed the top of his head lightly, thinking him asleep, but he turned and lifted the blanket and drew her in; later he put his arm around her and she tucked herself into his side and fell asleep with the reassuring scent of his deodorant close by.

Angela leaned forward on an elbow. "Now you need a quest," she said. "What'll it be?"

Cathy did have a quest in mind. It wasn't the kind where you go and find a thing, but one where you bring a thing with you and give it away. She told Pam and Angela about the Nice Young Man. "I'm not snatching anyone else's chalice, I just want to find him and hand over that bottle. Honest to god, the thought of it sitting in the closet for a month—I feel sick. Why didn't I just do it?" Because it was awkward, inconvenient, because she'd never seen this guy and it felt weird. What she didn't say was that, based on a wonky sense of retribution that was neither divine nor beneficent, her fear, increasingly, was that the longer she postponed thanking the Nice Young Man, the more likely Nan was not to get up and plug in the kettle in the morning.

It was about taking care of things, of herself, of the people who mattered to her, that's where Cathy was at; she wanted to smarten herself up, stop feeling out of breath at the top of the stairs; she wanted to feel less intimidated by the younger staff she managed, who all had the exact same straight hair going way down their backs, who arrived at work with gigantic coffees and led yoga classes at lunchtime and seemed to know far more than she did about absolutely everything and in the next moment to be so consumed by their own colossal ignorance that it was a wonder they could walk to their cars in the morning without tripping over themselves. Cathy felt surrounded and wanted to up her game, so she was embarking on a form of self-renewal that she hadn't clearly conceptualized but that did involve, for starters, the personal trainer and the tattoo. They'd encouraged her to get on Tinder, some of these women, but Cathy didn't understand Tinder (not that she would admit that, except to Angela and Pam, because they wouldn't understand it either) and she didn't want brief, agonizingly awkward hook-ups where she had to worry about whether it was okay to keep her socks on if her feet were cold. She honestly didn't give a shit whether she ever had sex again—she wanted someone to chat with while she made dinner, someone who would watch a movie in bed with her, someone who might notice if she croaked on a Friday evening and maybe prevent that eventuality by sending the paramedics over so her colleagues wouldn't be wondering mid-week why she hadn't got around to calling in sick. It wasn't about the physical piece, it was just about not feeling, when she brushed her teeth in the morning, that she was facing the day alone in her own head, and the next day, and all the days.

Pam, on the other hand, did want to have sex again. She wanted it as soon as possible, but Rod was always at work or tired, or his back hurt from leaning into cars all day long. Rod was important to her. She didn't want to do anything to jeopardize her relationship with her husband of many years, the father of her children, etc., etc. But she did think about Glenn quite often. They hadn't been close in school, but Glenn had swum across the river of early adulthood and emerged on the far bank strong, dripping, assured, yet attentive. He was unfailingly a pleasure to be with: warm, funny, kind. She respected his opinion. He listened to her. He never made her feel fat or stupid. She went to bed on a Sunday afternoon when Rod was watching the NASCAR and lay on her back; she closed her eyes and imagined Glenn standing beside her, unbuttoning his shirt.

And what of Trisha? Trisha was great. A lovely person. Pam didn't spend much time thinking about Trisha.

Pam was in the kitchen doing things with the cake dome. She had tried suggesting that Rod might ease back on work, with Luke out the door and the twins perhaps not far behind. Four children. Not that you'd give one back. You don't regret it. Not really. Although if she did regret one, it would be Travis. *Travis*. What had they been thinking? Did they imagine that baby was going to wear a

Stetson and head for Nashville? Some relative of Rod's. She must have had postpartum insanity. Four children was a lot. And Rod wanted to see them all through university, which could take forever, and she suspected that part of him liked it better at work, in the business he'd bought from his father, the smell of oil and the camaraderie of men. They had planned to hike a section of the East Coast Trail with Glenn and Trisha the previous fall; they were going to take a picnic and make a day of it, but Trisha ended up having to work and Rod had stomach flu, so Glenn and Pam had gone anyway, choosing a shorter stretch of coastline and ditching the picnic. She'd picked up ginger ale and plain salted crackers, set them on an end table within Rod's reach, brought over a bucket just in case, and tried not to skip out the door. Pam sensed she shouldn't be doing this, she shouldn't be enjoying Glenn's company so much, but she wanted to enjoy something. And she hadn't done a single thing wrong. It was a sunny, nearly windless fall day with the air coming in fresh and salty off the water.

"I can't believe we made her bake her own birthday cake," Angela was saying.

"Don't be foolish: which of us is going to make the best torte? No offence Ange, I know you're a whiz in the kitchen and everything, but."

"Okay guys," Pam said, "I'm not a hundred per cent sure how this is going to go." She slid plates in front of them, a wedge of dark chocolate torte sitting in raspberry sauce. A few flakes of toasted almond, a dollop of cream and a sprig of sage. Angela and Cathy made the appropriate noises and when Pam returned with her own plate, Cathy went to the sideboard and opened a drawer; she pulled out a single birthday candle, lit it from one of the tea lights, and pressed it into Pam's torte.

Pam drew a breath. One puff, but she'd misjudged the distance; the teeny flame bounced and jigged and waved, refusing to extinguish itself.

"Okay," Angela said. "Go team!" She and Cathy leaned in and the three of them breathed in together, pursed their lips, and blew.

"What was your wish?"

"I can't say."

On their hike, Glenn had stopped at the top of a rise to look out over the ocean; he was talking about a ship, but she couldn't see it. He'd slipped an arm around her shoulders and angled them gently; he'd leaned his face near hers so they shared a single perspective; he'd pointed. *There*, he said, and as they both looked out along his arm, his hand, his finger, she saw the ship in the distance heading away from the harbour, off to unknown waters.

In her head, Pam chose life over morality. She regretted in advance any ethical murkiness, but it couldn't be helped: time was short; they were all hurtling inexorably towards the finish line, and if an opportunity for joy presented itself, you should think yourself lucky.

The torte had a texture similar to that of cheesecake, only denser and more granular; it suggested a profound richness in the shadowy room. What with the wine and the awareness of all the years and the heady sense of connection, Cathy looked at the half-eaten slice of dessert on her plate and feared for a moment it might suck her in, fill her lungs with grainy chocolate velvet, envelop and suffocate her in its sumptuous darkness. She reached down and touched her ankle surreptitiously. *Brandish.*

There'd been a time when Cathy was sinking, after Don left. She went AWOL. Pam and Angela had had to stage an intervention. Don had taken the kids to Nova Scotia for a week; Cathy had missed a doctor's appointment, and the receptionist had called Don's cell thinking it was hers because the doctor wanted to discuss the bloodwork. The kids called her office and found out she hadn't been in for days, which never happened. Even Don was worried. So when Cathy didn't turn up in Bowring Park to walk the South Brook Trail with Angela and Pam as planned and she still wasn't responding to anyone, they drove to her house with the key Pam still had from when Cathy had been in Florida.

"Do you think she's gone out?" Angela said, watching Cathy's car in the driveway, hoping the door would swing open and Cathy would step out and say Boo!

"No," Pam said.

"Yeah." Angela lifted the knocker and hammered again, and rang the doorbell.

"Maybe we should just go, and call again later. Maybe her phone is dead."

"For days. And her work phone. And her landline. And her emails," Angela pointed out.

"She could have had a stroke." Pam tipped her head

back. "Cathy," she shouted, "we're coming in if you don't answer, okay?"

"Shelley in the departmental office was telling me the other day about a woman she'd met who had some kind of attack a few years ago, and if her son hadn't shown up.... I'm going to call again." Angela and Pam stood there by the door, hesitating, each looking at the other in the hope that she would say something confident, decisive, and obviously right. When that didn't happen, Angela pulled out her phone and called again.

A few minutes later, Pam was turning the key in the lock. "Hello?"

"Cathy?" Angela called. Angela and Pam looked towards Cathy's bedroom, down the hall to the right. The house was silent. Angela put a hand on Pam's arm as they approached the bedroom together. Pam knocked.

"Cathy," she said. "We need to know you're all right, okay? We're coming in."

She knocked again, louder.

After a few seconds Angela turned the handle and pushed the door. The room was dark. They could make out the bedding mounded on one side; there was no movement. Angela saw an arm dangling over the side; her eyes shot to Pam, who'd seen it too; they stood frozen for a moment, and then the bedding moaned.

"*Jesus,*" it said. "What the fuck are you guys doing here?"

Cathy had taken a sleeping pill for the first time in her life and it worked so well she knew she could never do it again. The unspeakable relief of waking up and realizing many hours had passed without requiring her attention. She ordered Angela to make coffee while she texted the kids to alert them to her continued existence. She plugged in her phone, which hadn't been working.

They stood in a row, leaning back against the kitchen counter, waiting for the perking glugs to stop.

"I can't believe you guys broke into my goddam house. Oh look, it's turning on now." Cathy started scrolling through the messages. "Oh my god. Oh."

"Only it's not really breaking in when you have a key for emergencies." Pam slid the spare key with its dangly Eiffel Tower along the counter.

"Well, before you go feeling too heroic over there, let's recall that it wasn't one." But Cathy slid the key back, lifted Pam's hand, and tucked it under her palm.

This was the story of their lives together: when one was floundering, the other two reached out and grabbed whatever part of her they could catch, they gripped hard enough to hurt, harder than that, they left marks, they hauled her along while she spluttered or puked or cried, they kept dragging until she was under her own steam again, and they did this with resolve and occasional bad temper, with humour and cursing, with a recognition of who was better at what and a full knowledge of everything that had brought them to this point, except the many things they'd forgotten, and most importantly they did it without hesitation; they did it with what they didn't usually think of as love because they didn't think about it much at all.

They had second helpings of torte and there was

scarcely a crumb left on the plates and now they were back in the living room with a fire log, having decaf and finishing off a bottle.

"I had a flight with Morgan," Cathy said, because she couldn't hold it in any longer, it flew out of her. "A fight. She's not speaking to me. Moved in with buddy. The boyfriend. Going to Alberta. She's pretty stubborn."

There was a silence.

"When?"

"Two weeks ago. Moved out of Don's too. They have the tickets booked."

Angela remembered the night Morgan was born like a video call that froze and pixelated. Cathy drinking herbal tea. Angela recalled the constant twisting, leaning on one armrest and then the other. That night Cathy walked home from Angela and Michael's. A few hours later she went to the hospital and produced Morgan a month early. Morgan nearly died and Cathy *very* nearly died. All that precariousness, Morgan might so easily not have made it. To think she had come through all that and whatever else life had to throw at her so far. She'd survived without catastrophe, without having been thrown off the rails by whatever happens to the brains of teenagers. It was such an unstable age, anything could happen. Cathy hadn't spoken to her parents for years, Angela remembered: she hadn't got on with her father and had eventually refused contact; he'd died not knowing what she looked like anymore. Her mother, Barbara, had faded gradually into the background of her life until she became entirely indiscernible. Nan and Harold were her people, Harold who'd hummed in the kitchen while he made them all blueberry pancakes after sleepovers, Nan who'd made sure Cathy had the yellow and the pink exercise books in the bookbag on Fridays, with fifty cents for ice cream. Sometimes when you pushed people away, there wasn't a way back to them even if you wanted to find it. No one was bringing those facts up just now, but they swam around below the surface of the conversation like a shark. Angela knew Cathy was afraid of losing the people she loved: if this wasn't the end of her relationship with Morgan, the important thing was that Cathy felt it could be. "Lotus," said Angela. "Blue Lotus?"

"Have some coffee, Ange," Pam said. "Cath, she doesn't mean it. It'll be, you know. Okay."

"She means where they work," Cathy said. "Morgan and the boyfriend. Jos—. Whasisname. Jeremiah. The Pink Delphinium. Restaurant. I don't even know when they're supposed to be leaving. Soon."

Morgan and Adam would never know how large they loomed in Angela's mind, and Pam's. Cathy's children were like giant balloons bobbing on the perimeter of the room. Same thing with Pam's boys and Olivia. The children of your best friends know who you are; they speak to you nicely. They have no clue how much their mothers have told you about them, how many zillions of details of their lives you remember that they did not retain beyond a day. They would be horrified. It was such a waste, really: they never knew how very ready you were to go to bat for them, defend them, protect them, stand up for them, no matter how huge or terrifying the opponent. Angela didn't care what Morgan thought of her (if anything), or how often (if ever). She, Angela, was not going to stand by and watch her destroy a relationship with a mother who adored her. Morgan would need that relationship later, and whatever Cathy had done, there was no point damaging both of them. Angela had had it with people being broken. She wanted them fixed.

"Let's go," said Angela. The others ignored her, or they didn't hear.

"What happened?" Pam asked.

"Damn," Cathy said, pouring a small slurp of coffee next to her cup, into the saucer.

It was hard, Cathy felt, to be the mother of adult (or nearly adult) children. You were interfering, trampling their independence, flaunting your ignorance, prejudice and general out-of-touchness, whatever you said. If you said *Hmm.* All you had to do was pour milk in your coffee in the morning for it to be construed as a negative comment. You breathe in and someone's saying *Whaaat?* What's your *problem???* Morgan was a good kid, but she had a will about her, a dark corner she let herself crawl into sometimes. Cathy wouldn't put it past her to move away and refuse all contact for months. And once you get to that point you might never go back. You convince yourself it's right, because you need to, because you've done it. Morgan was capable of that; it terrified Cathy. And in the middle of all that, because it was all knotted up together, she was thinking about the Nice Young Man, whom she could not, for some reason, stop thinking about, about that two-hundred-dollar brandy in the closet and the fact—because although Cathy was not generally superstitious, this loopy premonition had been hardening in the pre-dawn wanderings of her mind to the status of fact—that she needed to present herself and thank that man for keeping an eye and clearing Nan's steps, and the time for that was now.

"Dunno," Cathy said. She did know, sort of; it had started with the car. She knew Morgan had wanted the car for a weekend; she and Jeremiah had found a little house around the bay, they'd already booked it, it was clear that Morgan had expected to take Cathy's car, and this was what got Cathy's back up initially, the expectation—she hadn't expected to take Don's car, for example—and Cathy didn't want them to take the car, she wanted to use her car, which she paid for and maintained and put gas in, and mostly she didn't like the idea of them being out on the highway, she didn't know how much highway driving experience Jeremiah had, and if spring didn't start coming soon they'd be out on an icy highway and Cathy worried about this, about black ice, a speed that was a little over-confident, the car sliding first onto the shoulder and then through the guardrail and over an embankment and then ending up at the bottom, Morgan's face white, her eyes closed, a smear of blood on her forehead.

"Not just the car," she said. "It's never one thing, it's always everything."

"Talk to her, Cath," Angela said, gesticulating vaguely with her index finger.

"She won't talk to me."

"We need to do this." Angela had spent a lot of hours with Benjamin in the last couple of years. She would spend them all again tomorrow, she'd spend them a thousand times over, by god she loved that boy, and whatever he was up against, she would fight it. Or Rebecca, of course. Becca didn't seem to need defending at the moment but who knew what might happen, and Angela would have her daughter's back. And she would fight whatever Morgan was up against too, or Morgan's brother, Adam. She wanted a sword tattoo. And Pam's kids: Luke, if he needed backup, or Travis, or the twins, because the fellow-feeling of women was behind them now, the happy few, the band of mothers, they were invincible—Angela felt like the figurehead on the prow of a ship, confident and forward-moving; she would gather up the others and lead them forth into darkness and they would come through it erect and proud. "Let's.... A cab. They're working tonight, right, it's Thursday. Friday. Friday night. Is it Thursday? They take breaks."

"Ohhh, no," Cathy said. "Nope. Not going there. She'd kill me."

"We tell her you made us. Wait: I mean, we made you. Forced you. Right, Pam? Pam?"

Pam had been absorbed in the delicate pattern of small flowers on Cathy's china coffee service.

"Sorry?" said Pam.

"Yes! You say you're sorry. And you love her," Angela said.

"I don't care about the stupid car."

"Exactly. Tell her she matters to you," Pam encouraged.

"Course she matters! Obviously."

"Obvious to *her*," said Pam, who herself had a reached a point in her life when action needed to be taken, when enough time had been spent contemplating possibilities. Push had come to shove, and Cathy all of a sudden sounded resigned.

"It's not going to make things worse. Okay, but guys we're talking three minutes. I say *I love you, I'm really sorry.* Then we leave."

If Cathy seemed to hold out little hope of success, both Pam and Angela appeared infused with enthusiasm and were rising out of their seats: what they wanted was change for the better, and they wanted it so much they felt it surely must be achievable.

"Taxi, then...Pam?"

But Pam was already taking her phone out. "On it," she said, punching in numbers.

Cathy hesitated, but then she stood too. "Oh hell. You can only do your best, right? I'm trying." She picked up the bottle that had about one glass of wine left in it, sloshed the remainder among their glasses, and raised hers. "Hoping for the best."

"Wait!" Angela said. "The quest!"

"What—now?"

"We're a hundred and fifty. Let's do all the things. Where's the bottle?"

And instead of thinking this was a ridiculous idea, Cathy felt flooded with relief. Next thing they were in the hall pulling on their boots and Cathy was dragging a box out of the closet; through the window they saw a blob of yellow with two red lights appear in front of the house.

"Cab's here," said Pam, opening the door, and they poured out into the cold.

"Ange, I don't even know if she's working tonight, right?" Cathy was scarcely out the door and already plainly teetering in the direction of doubt. Angela was leading the way along the driveway and Pam positioned herself at the rear in case of stragglers.

"If not, well…we'll go somewhere for a nightcap."

They piled into the car and the driver headed for downtown. Cathy sat in front and chatted with Omar, who seemed glum: they were his third fare in an eight-hour shift, too many cars on the road, not enough business to go around, all the oil people had shipped out and no one was left to get a cab anywhere. He might go home after this. He probably wouldn't get another call all night. He'd only arrived at Christmas, to go to university, and hardly knew a soul. He'd never been cold in the spring before.

This would not do. The three mothers couldn't listen to an unhappy student far from his home without trying to do something about it. They had students of their own. Cathy's company often ordered cabs; she asked if they could request him. And if he didn't mind waiting, he could take them home again when they were finished downtown; it would only be a few minutes and they'd pay him for the wait. And they needed to go somewhere on the way home. So that was almost two more rides. Angela supervised a grad student who'd arrived recently and was looking for someone to hang out with; maybe she could put them in touch? Pam wondered if he knew about the new Middle Eastern mini-grocery, and it turned out he did not. And then he was pulling into a loading zone.

"We're just going to visit someone, it won't take long, okay?" Cathy said. "And if she's not working, we'll back in a jiffy."

But she was working. And so was the boyfriend. Angela shepherded the pack out of the taxi and along the road to the alley; they went to the end, where the garbage bins were, so they wouldn't been seen lurking from the street, and they'd stood for several minutes, whispering, wishing they still smoked, wondering how long they should wait, when the side door swung open and as if in a play—in fact, Cathy couldn't help thinking it: *Enter stage left*—out came Jeremiah in his grime-smeared whites with two bags of garbage. He turned towards the bins at the back of the alley and then he saw them and dropped the bags.

"Jesus fuck!" And, after a moment, "What are you doing here?" He peered at them. "Um, Ms. Norris?...Morgan's inside. I'll get—I'll tell her you're here." And before they could react he'd gone back in. Pam picked up the bags, carried them to the end of the alley and tossed them neatly into the bin, which had high walls; she bent her knees and did a slightly unsteady basketbally thing, and each bag sailed up and plopped down on the other side of the corrugated metal wall.

After a while the side door swung open again and out stepped Morgan, whose look of fury made even Pam and

Angela quail slightly. She was wearing a short black dress and black ballet slippers, standing in the trampled snow of the alley.

"What are you doing here? What's going on?"

Cathy started to reply but Angela cut her off.

"Morgan, this was me, okay? Not your mom. I made her come. She loves you and I know you love her too, and. Yeah. That's important." There was a pause.

Morgan's eyes scanned the semicircle of women. "You guys," she said, "have a nerve. Have you been drinking?"

"No," said Angela quickly. "It's Pam's birthday. A bit."

Cathy stepped forward. "Baby," she said, "sorry, we'll go." Morgan held the back of her wrist to her mouth as if she were physically trying to prevent herself from speaking to her mother, but the words burst out.

"You're goddam right you'll go. This is my *job*, Mom, where I *work*, like a grown-up. Can you imagine how you'd feel if I turned up at your job and had you paged, if I showed up there half-cut with Nala and Amber and started telling you what's important?"

"You can take the car," Cathy said. "I'm sorry I didn't say yes. I was worried."

Morgan made fists of her two hands and held them out at her sides, shaking them; she made a noise of strangled exasperation. "Oh my *god*, Mother, do you think that's what this is about? The car? It's not about the damn car. It's about trust, Mom. You don't mind trusting Adam, right? If Adam could drive and he'd asked for the car, you'd have helped him, wouldn't you?" Morgan had been ignoring

Pam and Angela, but now she turned to them. "She gets his breakfast every morning like he's the king or something. Do you know how old Adam is? He's sixteen, that's how old, he can get his own fucking breakfast."

"Morg, I put a few things out on the table, that's all. You don't even eat bre— "

"Mom, sometimes you cook him *eggs* before work in the morning."

Cathy stood there looking stunned, so Pam took a turn.

"I don't know what your mom did, honey. She might have done some things. We all do that. But you are everything in the world to her. Promise."

And whether it was Pam's calm sense of conviction or the fact that Morgan had sat on the dock at Angela's cabin when she was a child, desperately wanting to jump off but too afraid to try, and Angela had given her all the time she needed, encouraged, coaxed, caught her and applauded and lifted her up to do it again and again and again, or that Pam had brought her shopping for Mother's Day every year after Don left and given her money and they had smelled all the testers in The Body Shop and bought ice cream with sprinkles in a waffle cone, or that Morgan had finally said the beginning of what she needed to—whatever the reason, this seemed to bring them all to some sort of conclusion. Morgan smoothed the skirt of her dress and tucked some dark hair behind her ear.

"I have tables ready for their bills...." She surveyed them, shook her head. "You are a bunch of crazy old ladies." She didn't say it terribly nicely, but her tone had softened. "Go on home."

She turned her back and they walked towards the road, but they heard her voice calling out behind them: "Happy birthday, Pam!"

They did not go home.

"Well," Angela said as they scurried out of the alley towards Omar, "I think that was fairly successful."

"I don't know why she thinks I'm nicer to Adam." Cathy opened the door and slid into the passenger seat.

"Maybe you are," said Angela. "Maybe he's easier to be nice to. It's not something you can't change."

Pam said, "Maybe you should invite her out for lunch, just the two of you. Somewhere really great. Since she feels left out of breakfast."

Omar slid his phone into his pocket as they clambered in. "Hello again! Did you have a nice visit with your friend?"

"Okay, thanks," Cathy said. "It was fine. It was good, I think. Now." She twisted in her seat. "Are you guys sure you want to do this?"

"Brandish!" said Angela.

"Mullock Street, then, Omar, please." They trundled away from the harbour. The time downtown and the out-doors and cold air had sobered them up. They were heading uphill along a street with large homes on the right, set back behind gardens; to the left, a series of little roads spaced like the teeth of a comb, each tooth narrow and lined with rows of houses, tall and thin, all different heights and colours squished together. Omar turned up one of them and Cathy saw the neat navy blue of her grandmother's house, muted now between the streetlamps, the windows all dark except for the light over the front door—everything as it should be, her nan no doubt in bed for some time already. "Okay, wait, could we reverse a little? Wait now. One, two, three; it's that one." She pointed: burgundy clapboard with cream trim, and the picture window in the front was lit up; shadows moved on the other side of the blind. "Could you pull over there?"

"He's having a party!" said Pam.

Angela lolled forward to look past her. "Maybe he'll ask us in."

"Could you just pull over here and wait?" Cathy was unbuckling her seatbelt. "Omar, I'm just going to drop something off at this house here, it won't take long, so if you guys wouldn't mind waiting. No, Ange, we are *not* going in."

Cathy clutched the bag in front of her, climbed a few steps to the front door and knocked. When it opened, music flowed out and a man with short dark hair stood in front of her in jeans and a sweater. "Oh," Cathy said. Because she'd seen him before. And she became aware in that moment that Angela and Pam had not stayed in the car; they were standing a little back from her, one at each elbow. Not very far back. The man's face was neither welcoming nor hostile; his expression was even, he was waiting.

"I'm Cathy Norris," she said. "I'm really sorry to bother you so late." And she was now very sorry, thinking this had been a stupid idea—what had this poor guy done to deserve the three of them showing up unannounced at this hour like half-cut furies? They were all aware of the heat being sucked out into the street through the rectangle made by the open door, and he seemed to assess them and decide they did not pose a threat, because he moved back to let them in. Cathy stepped in carefully, avoiding a gym bag and some boots, Pam and Angela all smiles following her. The front door opened directly into the living room, where a handful of people were sitting around a coffee table that held a board game, a few beer bottles, and some snacks. They had all turned to watch Cathy and her posse. "My grandmother," Cathy said, "a few doors down, Eileen Norris—"

"Is she all right?" The Nice Young Man's forehead scrunched with concern.

"Oh yes, yes, it's not that. But I know you shovel her steps. Often. She really appreciates that. And so do I. I've been wanting to tell you that for a long time...." Cathy rummaged in her bag, explaining some more, and the man said it was really no trouble and Cathy apologized again for the late hour and the man pointed out that, as she could see, he was not in bed. Cathy produced the brandy that was expensive enough to come in a fancy box with antique-looking embossed swirly things on it, and he was clearly surprised and grateful, and invited her in for a beer. "And of course, your friends," he said, looking for the first time at Angela and Pam.

"Oh no, of course not, but thanks so much," Cathy replied, just as Angela was saying "That sounds nice."

"Really, it's fine, you're welcome to join us," he said.

Pam said, "Are you sure it's okay? I think there's a convenience store just over there, we could pick up some be—"

"Guys!" Cathy turned and flapped her hands towards

the door to usher the others out. Three vigorous, two-handed flaps. "Let's leave these people in peace."

"There's beer in the fridge. Come on in." The man was reaching for Angela's coat and Cathy glared at her. But in a small corner of her being, she too was pleased that the evening wasn't over yet.

Pam had been observing the cluster of friends as they watched Cathy and Anthony—because that, it turned out, was the Nice Young Man's name. They were contemplating the unfolding drama with interest and casting the occasional look at Ange and her. They were all younger than Pam, thirtysomethings, a guy with no hair, one with loads of it everywhere, and two women, a short one with a blonde ponytail and a rounder-faced, dark-haired one with a warm smile. The blonde one had stood up and taken a couple of steps towards the door at first, as if to fling herself between the man and the intruders should they offer any signs of belonging to a hostile army, but she soon moved back to her spot among the others, who didn't look alarmed or annoyed by the invasion at all; they seemed like the sort of people who'd have been pulling on their boots and mitts to help shove your car out of a snowbank.

"Oh my god!" Pam said. "Omar: he's still waiting!" Cathy rushed out to the car and talked through the window for a while and handed something over, and then she stood back and the car began to move. Omar pulled into a parking spot up the road and came and stood uncertainly in the porch, looking around, and Anthony approached and shook his hand.

"Hey man, come on in if you like." Omar surveyed the faces of the people in the living room and gave a shrug that suggested he didn't have much to lose, and soon he was settled with his three customers and Anthony and his Friday-night guests around the coffee table, some on the floor, and the electric fireplace made tall wisps of blue, yellow and red. The young people, as Pam thought of them, were trying to explain the rules of the game that had been interrupted. In the end, though, because it was easier, they decided to play two truths and a lie. Omar smiled and drank his ginger ale, and when the rules had been explained, he said he was here to study mechanical engineering, he didn't like chocolate ice cream, and he was from Tunisia.

Cathy was watching Anthony. She knew now where she'd seen him before. The twentieth of January was her nan's birthday. The afternoon before, Cathy had stopped at the supermarket to pick her up some flowers. Nothing extravagant, her grandmother wouldn't approve of that, and she had taken her out for lunch on the weekend anyway— just some carnations: a bit of life and colour, and they lasted well. She'd stood at the express checkout behind a man in a long black wool coat. There had been a ping and everyone in the queue had reached for their phones. They'd laughed at one another. *Here we all are*, their expressions said, *stuck to these ridiculous things all the time, and we don't even know who's getting a message.* The man in front of Cathy pulled his phone out of his coat pocket. He was a nice-looking man, Cathy had registered that, with a serious face, and he typed in a couple of letters. Excuse me, he said, sliding past her, and she realized he must have forgotten something, or maybe his wife was sending him a reminder to pick up baby food, and his cart sat there, the asparagus, the cherry tomatoes, the frozen shrimp. He never came back.

That man had been Anthony. And she knew now, sitting across from him—she had noticed the knee of the ponytailed one, Jessica, beside him, that knee just barely touching his, almost not touching but touching enough that someone could have shifted an inch if they hadn't wanted to feel a knee there—Cathy knew where the ping had come from, she could see Anthony walking away; in her mind's eye she followed him home, his quick stride alongside the hockey rink, the sound of his breath in the winter air, his fingers twisting the key and the ponytail appearing out of nowhere, from one of the cars in the street, pushing him in through the door, their movements quick and close. That was what had happened, Cathy felt convinced, while the shrimp defrosted in the cart and her nan put water in a vase; she looked at Jessica and then directly at Anthony as if she were searching for the truth, and he saw her look and lowered his eyes and she was sure.

"Of course he likes chocolate ice cream, that's foolishness, come on now, Omar," Jessica was saying. She was teasing him, drawing him out; she was funny and he liked the attention. "So either it's not Tunisia or it's not mechanical engineering. What other kinds are there? Chemical?"

"I don't know if they can do chemical here," someone said. Everyone at the table was watching Omar in a tilted-head, friendly-scrutiny sort of way.

"Okay..." Laura said thoughtfully. She was the dark-haired one. "Going out on a limb here, but I wonder if you're Tunisian. There aren't many Tunisians here—no offence if you actually are one—so it's more likely you're from somewhere else."

Omar nodded. "I grew up not far from Beirut," he said.

"I don't believe it!" Jessica said. "You haven't been doing it right. You've been eating the wrong kind. We're going to have to get you something decent. Have you had Häagen-Dazs? Ben and Jerry's? Have you had Moo Moo's?"

"I have not had Moo Moo's," he confessed.

"Well my son, we're going to change that. We'll go to Moo Moo's next week and you can try a few and see if you don't change your mind."

Omar clearly didn't know whether to take her seriously, whether he'd actually be expected to show up for ice cream the following week, but it was seeming increasingly likely that he would and that he was up for that, and Dustin (Hair and No-Hair were actually Dustin and Alex) expressed a preference for peanut butter ripple, and then they were on to Angela, and of course it turned out that she had relatives who lived in the mountains not so far from Omar's hometown, and some comparing ensued and then it was her turn. Angela was no longer checking her phone, Cathy noticed; she'd stopped doing that some time ago, although it was no doubt in a pocket and turned on. Ange was pausing, thinking about what she would say, and Cathy was putting her money on something about Benjamin, and then something inconsequential, and finally maybe a work-related thing—some factoid about wildlife.

"I am very worried about my daughter." That's it, Ange, heave it out of you, Cathy thought: it was good for her to have this opportunity to admit it to kind strangers. And she'd said *daughter*—to protect Benjamin, probably. So that was the lie. The crew around the coffee table took this in with solemn and respectful silence. "I once met Benny from ABBA."

What the fuck, thought Cathy. That's the wine talking.

"One lie." She nudged Angela. "Two truths."

Angela gave her a gentle eyeroll. "I *know*, Cath."

Could this be true? Could she have known Angela for all these years and not known she'd met Benny from ABBA? Impossible. Cathy looked at Pam, who raised her eyebrows. Was Angela confused? She didn't look confused. She looked as if she was having the time of her life. But they had known Ange forever, they knew her all to pieces, where would she have met Benny from frigging ABBA on some occasion she'd kept silent about for the rest of her life? They knew everything about one another. They'd slipped past the bouncers in university on a Friday night and got drunk in the Orange Room and flung their bodies around to "Back in the USSR"; they'd studied, among other things, terrestrial ecology (Angela), T. S. Eliot's *Four Quartets* (Cathy) and Advanced Spreadsheet Modelling (Pam); they had graduated and got jobs and survived the early stages of relationships and marriage. Each would happily have eviscerated a husband with bare hands in the following circumstances: when she was peeing on a pregnancy test stick in the bathroom of the Duke of Duckworth while her husband drank with the crowd upstairs, oblivious, unburdened by any smidgen of knowledge or responsibility; awake in bed at five a.m. wondering if he was coming home from the party or had left it with his colleague Linda; when he'd said something mean and sarcastic at supper, in front of others, that made it clear he thought of her chiefly with contempt and could no longer be bothered to conceal that fact. They had sat with the very same husbands on the couch at night laughing about things nobody else would understand or find funny; they had seen small gestures of kindness and appreciated them; they had left a funeral and taken a husband's arm and clutched it gratefully on the way to the car. They'd moved away for a year or five—Toronto, Vancouver, Calgary—and come back again. They'd built professional lives and raised their children. And yet somehow, half a century in, thanks to privilege, good luck, and Medicare, they saw each other regularly; they had, this very evening, eaten and drunk and celebrated and traipsed around the downtown on good deeds and had a propitious encounter and were now winding up their evening in the company of engaging and lovable strangers. But...Benny? Jesus. Cathy's gaze rose over the top of the conversation and the out-loud musings of the assembled as to the probability of the various statements; her gaze arched over the little hubbub and touched down on Pam, and Pam shrugged.

Angela was listening to Laura, who was telling her in a side conversation that she, Laura, had a few friends who had gone through tough times, some pretty serious stuff, when they were around the age of Angela's daughter, and a bit older—in case that was the true statement, Laura added carefully—and it had been hard but they were okay now, and although Laura obviously didn't know anything about Benjamin, she somehow conveyed the sense that she was a possessor of wisdom, and Angela drank in that confidence because it was what she needed now more than anything: hope, she could taste that hope, it was like an energy bar when you were out doing fieldwork and forgot your lunch. It would keep her going.

And Pam was thinking that Alex looked just a little like Glenn, if you superimposed close-cropped greying hair and reading glasses; there was something in the face, and she too was wondering about Benny and where that had come from, and she could see Cathy across the table and noticed something about her: she thought that Cathy was actually looking a tiny bit muscly, a bit more of a driving force, physically speaking: good for her and her gym-going, and Pam might decide to get in on that, it was use it or lose it and she had definitely lost a lot but there was no point giving up, she could go to a few classes, heft a few weights (*Brandish!*); soon the snow would be melting off the trails and it would be hiking weather. She could use some of it.

"My uncle has a cabin near Foxtrap," Anthony was saying, which Pam decided was a lie and Angela and Cathy felt to be true. "I talked on the phone yesterday with a guy on the Falkland Islands." Pam believed this immediately, and so did Angela. "I. I would like to have a child." All eyes were on him now, and Cathy's went straight to the two knees resting against each other.

The three of them had started saying *I love you* to each other in the last year, at the end of a walk or a phone call; it was new and a little awkward, and they said it deliberately, loudly enough that there could be no doubt; they wanted to say it, wanted to hear it, wanted it to be known, and if the last two decades of their lives had been spent building their families and their careers, putting things in the oven and taking them out again, wiping away blood and kissing and sending off, getting up in the night and bringing a glass of water, touching a hot forehead, shaking pills out of the cotton fluff at the mouth of the bottle, picking up and dropping off and working late and birthday cakes and basketball and parent–teacher interviews and applying for promotion and delivering the forgotten trumpet for band and worrying when someone missed their curfew and wasn't answering, and losing one's temper, fuming and crying and hugging and more meals, and still more—if those were the constituent components of their thirties and forties, two decades devoted to giving and giving and trying and making and washing and trying harder, maybe this new decade would be something different, maybe it would be about love, loving themselves and each other and others besides, maybe it would be about having the freedom, the space to put their heads up and look around and notice, about loving generously and widely and well. They already loved all of these new friends— who were warm and welcoming and seemed unencumbered by perimenopausal fluctuations or writhing self-doubt—and if their collective powers allowed it, they would spin a future for Anthony; they would weave a blanket of safety and happiness and love for his baby. They felt confident, the three of them, in this moment, that they could do it. They knew it. Right now, they could do anything.

GRAPES

BRANDON'S MOM TURNED off the road and onto a track by the sign that said Community Garden; she parked at the side, on the grass. They'd come to help his grandfather dig over his allotment. He followed his mom along the path by a shed. The door stood open; as they passed, he saw a rolled-up hose and a pitchfork in the gloom and smelled a murky garden smell. Even though there was frost in the evenings now, he could feel the sun on his back, and the earthy shed air that drifted out still seemed to hold a promise of unfurling, of blooming and transformation.

The garden was a field divided into rectangular plots marked out with string tied to sticks in the corners. Some were covered in complex low structures that looked like paramilitary training grounds for very small humans, or possibly fairies: rows of stakes, a series of semicircular hoops, frames like mini volleyball nets for who knows what. There were trenches and black cloth and the odd chair or metal drum.

At first his grandfather didn't seem to be there, but then his mom called out a greeting and a figure straightened and waved. Even in his eighties, Brandon's grandfather was tall and strong, broad-shouldered. He'd been shovelling earth into a wheelbarrow, Brandon saw as they approached. Pop knew what to put in the soil to make vegetables grow. He could make things work when they didn't want to, like the lawnmower or the snowblower. He was handy with drywall, good with a saw. Gram was always trying to get him down off a ladder—he'd say Just a minute now, I'm almost done.

It would be a fair bit of heavy digging, Brandon had been told. He'd asked his mom if she wanted him to find a buddy to come and help, but she'd said they'd be fine with the three of them. He was happy to help his grandfather, but he hoped it wouldn't take too long. Some of the guys were probably heading to the park before supper. He pulled his phone out of his pocket and had a quick look, but there were no messages.

Pop did one more shovelful, stamping his foot down on the edge of the thick steel so it chopped through the dirt. The shovel's blade was shaped almost like a heart, and the point penetrated the earth first, guided by Pop's boot. They needed to pull up all the weeds and vegetation on the surface, spread rotten leaves on top of the ground, and dig them in for next year. Brandon's grandfather had taken everything up except the last leeks and parsnips, which meant that everything except that final row needed to be dug over. It was looking like a long afternoon and he wondered whether to put a note in the group chat to say he didn't know if he'd make it to the park. He and his mom were pulling on heavy cotton gloves and his grandfather was beginning to issue specific instructions when a man ambled over from a neighbouring rectangle.

"How're your carrots, Ed?" the man said. "Got the fly?"

"Not too bad; I had them covered," said Brandon's grandfather. "How about you?"

"Aah, they're full of fly. Black with it." Brandon tried to catch his mother's eye to see if they could get started or if they had to wait for the man to finish talking with his grandfather, which could take, by Brandon's estimation, about a hundred years. But she was looking at the man and smiling sympathetically. He thought about nudging her, but he was a little afraid to get her attention. Brandon's mom had a way of training her focus on a prioritized sequence of areas needing attention. If he hopped into the field of her radar, her gaze might slice into the core of him like Pop's shovel going into the ground, and he didn't know how she might react to what she saw in there.

"I was going on holiday," the man continued. "Didn't have a chance to cover them, and when we got back it was too late." He examined the row of leek and parsnip and nodded approvingly. "I tried companion planting," he said. "Waste of time. Anyway, I can't stand marigolds."

The man and his wife, Brandon learned unwillingly, had been on an Alaskan cruise out of Vancouver. He took a few steps away and started pulling up some straggly stalks, hoping they were weeds. The man had moved on to a new topic: his grapes. He'd seen them grown in the Mediterranean.

"They cut them right back over there, boy, there's not much left to that stalk at the end of the season." Next thing, the man was strolling over to the greenhouse.

"Pop," Brandon said. "Those leaves—" But Brandon's mother and grandfather were following the man.

He got his phone out again. *Not sure if I can make it*, he typed, but he didn't hit Send.

Brandon's grandfather and his mom were trying the grapes and making approving noises; the man held out his hand and Brandon didn't want any but he picked a couple off the bunch to be polite. He wasn't sure who would be at the park, whether Seamus might be there, and he was about to say something to his mother in a tone he might feel bad about later, not rude exactly but maybe bad-tempered, to remind her he was there, because he was sick of standing around waiting for them, but then he heard a word that made him prick up his ears. That word was *rototiller*.

"Now Ed," the man was saying, "you don't need to dig all that over—I'm coming up with the rototiller next week."

"Are you really," said Brandon's grandfather. The sun came out from behind a cloud and tossed a stripe of light over the yellowy orange trees behind the compost pile.

A couple of hours of digging vaporized instantly, like in *Overlord III*: pull the trigger and zap. The task was reduced to scraping the weeds off the surface and tossing them into a wheelbarrow, which would hardly take any time. Grape

Man ambled back to his plot, but by this point he could've stuck around longer, as far as Brandon was concerned. He could've taken his sweet time.

Brandon was glad now that he hadn't asked Seamus if he could come and help. There was no need. Also, he wasn't sure if they were close enough friends for that, for a family Saturday thing, he didn't want him to think it was weird. His mom was chatting with his grandfather, but she was whipping that hoe around too. They were underway, and Pam didn't mess around when there was a job to be done. He might even have a chance to get a shower before the park. Brandon grasped two fistfuls of yellowing vegetation and tossed them in a pile.

A man in muddy jeans and a T-shirt appeared behind his grandfather. Brandon hadn't seen him earlier. He could have wandered out of the woods. "Ed," the man said, but Brandon's grandfather didn't hear. "Hi Ed," he repeated.

"Dad," Brandon's mom said, and indicated the man.

Brandon powered along the rows of the plot, hauling weeds and flinging them on the pile, imagining he was laying waste to the enemy's crops.

"How you been? I know you had a little spell there a while back."

Pop's spell had been a quadruple bypass the previous summer that kept him in hospital for the better part of two months and left him looking strained and gaunt for a year, during which time, Brandon had heard his mother say, all the people from the other plots had watered and weeded and generally tended his rectangle, in addition to sending pictures so he could see how things were growing.

"Fit as a fiddle now," Pop said, and the man said a buddy of his had the same thing happen, fifty-three years old, now he was a big boy but still, bang, just like that; good thing he went to the hospital, he thought it was something he ate.

"You're looking good," the man said. "Let me know if you need a hand with anything."

There was something in his voice that Brandon recognized but couldn't quite identify, and it rolled around in mind as he pulled at a lacy weed with shallow roots that sat on the soil like a floppy hat. He tugged at the green frills and then caught the roots with a fork. That thing he'd heard, Brandon realized after a few moments, didn't reside in a particular word; it was the man's tone. It was a loving tone. The thought insinuated itself in among his other thoughts and he wrinkled his face with hostility at the weirdness of it, but that was it: a subspecies of love, more precisely, which was a real and felt kindness. His phone played the four seconds of a Drake song that meant a text had come in, and he pulled off his glove and reached into his pocket. *Yo*, the text said. *Comin to the park or what?* It was Seamus.

Brandon gripped the handles of the wheelbarrow and lifted them as if someone were watching and he wanted them to see the strength in his arms, which was considerable because he worked out a lot.

"I'm just gonna go empty this," he said.

· · · · ·

During the Wisconsin stage of the Pleistocene, glaciers covered the entire island of Newfoundland. They advanced and retreated, scraping off topsoil like Brandon's mother's spatula pulling buttercream from the sides of a mixing bowl, sprinkling stones over the ground. The earth is rocky and acidic, the growing season short. And yet Grape Man had held out his hand to Brandon with a bunch of tiny globes in his palm, each one smaller than a pea, scarcely bigger than the couple of seeds inside. They were a translucent green that seemed to be lit from within, alive and beautiful.

BABY WHALES

GAME ON

OF COURSE THEY were probably not going to win the Senior Skip Scavenger Hunt. But they might. They had team shirts and as good a shot at it as anyone. The photo on the front of the shirts had been taken at a sleepover the previous weekend; it featured the four of them and, in the middle, Chloe's white stuffed whale, which had a friendly smile and was called Raphael.

Alyssa, Erin, Chloe, and Becca had taken over Alyssa's family's car. Alyssa and Becca were the only ones who knew how to drive, and Becca's mom needed her car to take Becca's brother to an appointment. Alyssa had on giant brown sunglasses, plus black leggings and a mocha cardigan that swished down around her knees. Her brown hair hung out the window so she looked like a movie star. She flicked her hair back and stuck an elbow out into the cool morning air.

At eight o'clock, cars were already lining up, engines running, except the ones whose drivers had turned off the engines because idling is worse for emissions than driving, which had been pointed out in the instructions on social media. Students with bright orange vests and clipboards wove through the parking lot, leaning into driver-side windows. They scribbled things on the clipboards and handed pieces of paper through the windows and smacked the roof once or twice in a way that said *You're good to go*. And then each car revved up and burned out of the lot.

Liam Bonia in his orange vest bent himself in the shape of a shepherd's crook to talk to Alyssa at the wheel. "Any drugs in here?" he asked, looking stern, and Alyssa stammered a surprised No! but Chloe said What kind? even though they'd never even bought decongestant.

Liam laughed and said, "Kidding, I feel like Border Patrol here: see your passports, haha," and it was super awkward because he and Erin had dated for a while, before Erin started seeing Alyssa. But now Liam was talking to Alyssa and Chloe in front, and he probably didn't even see Erin because she was behind with Becca, her hood pulled way up, slouching under a blanket and a couple of backpacks. Liam looked through the spreadsheet on his clipboard, checked them off, and handed Alyssa their list of challenges.

"Everything has to be documented on one phone: photo and video," he said. "Your official start time is 8:17 a.m. Game on!" He tapped the hood of the car twice and said "Hey Erin" and turned away.

Erin hadn't been part of the friend group for long. She didn't know Becca or Chloe very well: she'd gone to elementary and junior high in the west end. Apart from the sleepover the previous weekend, this would be their biggest stretch of time together, so it was sort of a test to see if they'd like her, to see if she'd be accepted. Not that anyone had said anything like that, of course. Alyssa would be deciding whether Erin was really dating material. They were all pretty geeky, that was their thing, but Alyssa ranked several notches higher on the coolness ladder and maybe dating Erin would feel like too much of a come-down. By the end of the day, Erin sensed, she'd receive a kind of evaluation. She imagined the others standing in a row, each holding up a sign with Pass or Fail written on it. Because none of this was explicit and because they were all in any case far too nice to be thinking in these terms, nothing would be said directly, but there might be a small clue, a reference to a future event with the implication that she would be there or, if things didn't go well, a conversation in which she didn't really know what was going on but no one bothered to explain because whether she understood or not wouldn't be important.

They were geared up to pick a challenge off the list and fling themselves face-first into it with every bit of energy, determination, and intelligence they possessed, which was a not at all insignificant amount, but on mature reflection they decided to go and have a coffee and strategize the fuck out of the list first because frankly strategizing was what they were most awesome at. And because, since it was an early start, no one had eaten breakfast. And also because Alyssa said she wasn't driving anyone anywhere until she got coffee.

FASHION SHOW

THEY HAD TO stage a fashion show. They had to curate a dramatic outfit each and model it on video. Every outfit had to be partly orange. And they didn't have all day. Alyssa swung the car into a parking space at Frugal Fashion and jammed her foot on the brake so the four of them bobbed forward and then back all together, like the heads of chickens.

"Guys, listen," Chloe was saying urgently, consulting the list, "we have to get video of one of us touching someone's beard, so if you see any bearded dudes who don't look too grouchy, let's go for it." They were doughnutted, caffeinated, ready for action; they sprang out of the car and ran to the store entrance.

Erin dove into the formal section, which made her think of Liam one year earlier at the spring concert. The chamber choir set had gone really well. The auditorium had been filled with friends and families; there was applause and cheering, and Mr. Cooper sent them back to the music room to wait until the jazz band was done. The jazz band was the last act and after that they were to go out to the lobby and find their parents. So everyone was milling around the music room in tuxedos and black dresses, and she sat at the piano and started to play the song she had just accompanied onstage. Hardly even playing it, just touching the keys. Two of the girls and Liam had sung solos, one verse each, and the choir came in on the chorus.

She chose the piano bench because she didn't want to be standing around feeling awkward in one of the little clusters, not knowing what to say; she didn't know if she would have a cluster or if anyone would want her in theirs, or if she would end up standing alone next to someone else's cluster like the big dead plant by the window. That would be the worst thing, being the one dead plant, or maybe the worst thing would be joining a cluster and, in an effort to participate in the conversation and possibly to be funny, saying something that came out louder or more outrageous than she'd meant and seeing them all look briefly horrified and then cover it up.

So she took refuge in something purposeful, an activity for which it was normal to be alone, until Liam came and sat beside her on the piano bench. He slung his knees under the keyboard and tugged neatly on his trouser legs, and she scooched over a little to make room for him. Her black dress was off the shoulder and she felt the fabric of his tux jacket scuff up against her arm as he settled in, and that scuff shot into her like a vaccine against loneliness, against sadness, against anything bad; she felt that tuxy shoulder course through her arm and into her core and pulse through her organs; she arrived at the verse and he leaned into her a little as he sang, and gradually everyone in the room stopped talking and they all joined in on the chorus. At the end they clapped and he turned his face to hers and smiled, and she smiled back.

That had been the beginning of her and Liam, who was

actually a really good guy, for whom she now felt a twinge of nostalgia and after whom she had been half-tempted to call out *Hey Liam!* from the back of the car, only that would have been totally embarrassing, since she'd been hiding back there. And now she was sort of dating Alyssa, who Erin strongly suspected had thrown up her chocolate-dipped doughnut in the bathroom before they left the coffee shop. It wasn't about looks or being thin, Erin knew that: it was about being able to control one small thing—having the power to make that sweet, greasy ring disappear with a single flush, as if it had never existed.

Erin whipped through the prom dresses and found Alyssa in Ladies' Knits. Clothes stores were triggering for Alyssa. She was standing on the other side of the rack from Erin, flipping the hanger after she'd looked at each sweater. There was a little scrape of the hanger on the metal rail each time—scrape, scrape, scrape. Erin could hear her breathing.

Erin said, "Lyss, we'll be out of here in ten minutes."

Erin had visited Alyssa in the fall in the psych ward, which is where the eating disorder patients go. Alyssa's mom had brought Erin to the unit and told her to text when she wanted to go home. You had to be buzzed in and out. A man and a girl went in ahead of Erin and at the desk they searched the girl's gym bag. The girl was wearing a baggy green hoodie and combat boots and you could see a corner of white bandage poking out by her wrist.

Alyssa hadn't looked like one of those girls on Insta-gram who post pictures of their matchstick legs and get thousands of likes, that wasn't the point, but she hadn't looked great. Her hair usually fell in glossy brown waves, but it had been stringy, and her face had looked pale and kind of yellow-orange in places. Alyssa's room had her name written in cheery colours on a mini whiteboard by the door, and someone had drawn a flower beside it. She told Erin you weren't allowed to close the door all the way in the bathroom, and one of the nurses stood outside waiting for you. The two of them had gone to the lounge, which had chunky coffee tables and blocky couches, brightly coloured walls with uplifting messages stencilled on them.

Alyssa said, "That's so bogus: Ghandi never said 'Be the change you want to see.'"

They'd worked on a puzzle for a while. They both liked puzzles, but a thousand pieces took too long and five hundred was too easy. Alyssa said she couldn't pay attention to anything for long. They talked about school, and Alyssa told Erin about the school in the unit. "The teacher posts really great chem notes. I'll show you." She opened up her laptop and turned it towards Erin and somehow the search history came up by mistake. It was all food: recipe after recipe after recipe, lemon meringue pie, extra cheesy lasagna, brownies, casseroles. Alyssa snapped the laptop closed.

After a while the nurse came with a snack and sat a little distance away. It was clear she had to stay and make sure Alyssa ate the snack, which was a vanilla pudding and two arrowroot cookies, and Alyssa said, "Maybe you should text my mom now," because her mom was waiting downstairs in the coffee shop. When Erin left, Alyssa was trying not to let her see that she was crying because she didn't want to eat the snack.

Alyssa was doing much better now—clothing stores didn't bring out the best in her, that was all. Chloe came scampering down the stairs, brushing hair off their face. Chloe's hair was light brown; it had been long but was now shaved on one side and the back; the top swooped down and sideways over their right eye, as if they were hiding, peeking out from behind that little waterfall of hair, which sometimes they were. "Guys," Chloe said, "come on up, it's time to shoot!"

"Our final contestant," Chloe said, "the amazing Becca, in a leopardskin coat and orange sneakers!" Becca was short and muscular, with a bleached-blonde rugby buzz cut, and after taking a few staged steps towards Chloe and the camera, she tripped on the hem of the floor-length coat and crashed into Alyssa.

On the video later they would see Becca lurching, Alyssa tipping, their mouths opening in shock, Erin grabbing Alyssa, the three of them swaying in a little pod, hanging on and righting themselves. By then the camera was shaking with Chloe's laughter and the picture zipped all over the place as the others reached for Chloe and pulled them into the scrum, and they hung on to one another for dear life because they were laughing almost too hard to stand up.

Seconds later they were ripping the gear off and running down the stairs to hang it back up—because, despite moments of rebellion, they were fundamentally obedient and good citizens, even when the clock was ticking. They wanted to do the right thing, to be decent people, to work hard and be kind to their fellow humans—and also animals of course. They wanted to make the world a better place, if it wasn't altogether too late for that, which it probably was. They were prepared to give it their very best shot.

ALREADY WEIRD

BOLTING FOR THE exit, they lurched to a halt near the check-outs because they'd all seen the same thing: Bearded Dude on the middle cash. They went into a huddle by Men's Jackets.

"Becca," Alyssa said, "is that your brother?"

Chloe glanced at Becca and jumped in: "No, but you're right, he looks a bit like him."

Becca's brother was sick. Becca had got up to go to the bathroom in the middle of the night and nearly stepped on her mother, who was lying on a yoga mat on the floor outside Ben's room. Half-asleep in the dark, she'd seen a shadow near her foot, and then the shadow had moved and grown and turned into an eel and then a human being and Becca had screamed. Her mother had stood and hugged her and stroked her hair and said Shh. Once her parents had to take her brother to the hospital in a hurry and they forgot about her. She went home after school and no one appeared, there were no messages and suppertime came and went, and around ten o'clock at night they came through the door and her mom said "Oh my god, Bec," as if she were surprised to see her, surprised she lived there too. "I forgot about you, my honey," her mom said. "I'm so sorry." Becca could see that, although she would never have admitted it, would have lied fiercely to avoid admitting it, her mother had not just forgotten to call or let Becca know she'd be on her own for supper. Becca's mother had forgotten her altogether, forgotten briefly that she existed, and the surprise was the shock of being reminded, of having let something of this magnitude slip away.

Becca's mother had lost weight and she would have looked nice if her face hadn't looked so hard all the time, like a plastic mould of her real face, and sometimes in the kitchen in the morning her mother would say What time is rugby today? and Becca would say Four o'clock at Wishingwell, and three minutes later, her mother would say What time is practice today, Bec? and she'd say It's at four, Mom, and before Becca had left for school her mom would say Beckster, is there rugby today?

You can't just go up and touch someone's beard, it's creepy, it's beard assault, especially if you're filming it. They wouldn't be comfortable with that. But no one wanted to ask him. And it might be weird if he let them touch his beard and then left without buying anything.

"The thing is," Erin pointed out, "it's already weird."

It fell, somehow, to Chloe, to buy something and ask him at the checkout.

Chloe grabbed a ninety-nine-cent bracelet off the jewellery rack; it was a bunch of shiny green irregular plastic rocks strung on elastic; it was junky, but they liked how the green wasn't one single green but a constellation of flickering greens that shifted as it moved through light.

Chloe stood in the lineup that thank god had only one person ahead, because already they had spent too much time in the store and the other teams would be gaining on them.

Chloe felt sick at the idea of asking this guy. They didn't know what to say and they could feel their toes bunching inside their red high-tops. Maybe the woman in front with the striped baseball baby jumpsuit and the duck board book and the Nanny's Little Angel fleece blanket would take a while, would take forever, even if it meant losing. Chloe could make a chart of what they wanted to say, could draft an essay and then edit it and submit it to the cashier and get a 97 per cent and probably win a Best Essay prize for it, but opening their mouth and doing it on the spot was not cool, very much not their skill set. The friend group always ordered pizza online so no one had to talk to anyone.

The woman was handing over a ten-dollar bill now and Chloe was clutching the bracelet in its clear stapled plastic bag with the ninety-nine-cent sticker on it, and the plastic was damp. If Chloe felt nervous now, if their hand was sweating, would they sweat more, would Bearded Dude notice they were sweating? The dampness was a signal, a warning message that said *Hello there: for your information, things aren't going well and might get worse— please monitor this situation carefully and prepare for emergency intervention.* What if he didn't like being asked, what if he got angry, would he shout, would he call for the manager, would the others come as backup or would Chloe have to face the situation alone?

When Chloe started to sweat, sometimes things got worse, not always but sometimes. There was a cold whoosh that started at the top of their head, prickled down their scalp and rushed over their body. They knew what to do for a panic attack—they needed to breathe slow and deep, be grounded, feel their feet on the floor, maybe sit and put their head down—but that would mean getting out of the line, fuck, there wasn't time for that, and the guy was giving the woman change now, fuck fuck, and it was almost their turn, fuckety fuck; his name was Dustin, it said so on his name tag and fuck he was turning to them and they didn't feel good at all, dizzy and sick, and he smiled and fuck they thought they might faint *right now*, oh *fuuuuck*—they reached out for the counter to steady themself and he said, "Hi, do you want to touch my beard?"

"Umm..." Chloe said, gripping the counter. "Yes? Please? If you're, like, chill with that. Really, yes. That's—awesome, thanks a lot!"

He said, "You can film it if you want, you're my third group this morning."

Chloe turned to where the other three had been lurking by the door, trying to look both nonchalant and purposeful, as if waiting by the exit in a second-hand clothing store that smelled of dust was something you did only if you were outstandingly cool, unhurried, if you were unbothered by anything, if you were unspeakably bored and possibly secretly wealthy, if your default way of being in the world was lounging, probably by a pool, but not the kind they were familiar with, the kind packed with younger siblings having lessons and two-year-olds with water wings and stubby little feet shivering on the deck: the other kind of pool, which they would like to get to know. In truth they had not been markedly successful in projecting that look, but never mind, here they were, running up with the phone, and Chloe reached over and patted Dustin's beard and he grinned at them.

Chloe said, "Thanks, Dustin, you're the best," but by that point he was reaching for the painted flowerpot and Corningware casserole dish of the next person in line and they weren't even sure if he'd heard, and Erin grabbed Chloe's arm and said *Quick!* and when Chloe turned they saw the doors of a car out front burst open and four identical green T-shirts fly out and jog to the entrance.

They flung themselves under the exit sign and into the car and four doors slammed, and they went "Holy shit, OMG, Chloe, that was amazing, that was soooo awesome, how did you do that, what did you say to him?"

Chloe just said, "Oh you know," in a casual way, but they felt like one of the tie-dyed T-shirts everyone had to make in Positive Living, with orange and red and yellow streaks radiating outwards—the whole inside of Chloe's body felt like that circle of colourful happiness. Chloe felt outstanding.

"Did he say his *third* group this morning?" Becca asked. Alyssa hit the pedal and zipped out into the traffic fast enough to get honked at.

"Dick!" she yelled.

SCREW IT

TIME HAD ALWAYS been slow. They'd spent their lives waiting: for someone to buy the good kind of peanut butter, for the last desultory days of the school year and the almost-empty building with no one in a hurry, for a parent to stop being angry, for a call from the person whose name on the phone made them hold their breath.

But all of a sudden life had sped up: they needed to move faster, tick off more tasks, tick tick tick.

In the supermarket parking lot Becca juggled three tissues and Chloe ate a lime (but not the peel, it didn't say anything about peel); Erin gobbled a jalapeño and Alyssa photographed a grumpy firefighter. A boy in a hoodie ran past them in the lot carrying a lime in his hand and a bag of dog biscuits in the other. Then it was back in the car, headed for Chloe's place. Alyssa said, "Hey, was that Samir with the lime?"

Chloe said, "Guys, that lime was the sourest thing ever, the inside of my mouth is wrinkled. My teeth feel funny, do you think that's okay?"

It had been Samir, and although Becca didn't answer Alyssa's question, she thought about him a lot. She wasn't always sure if it was him she was thinking about or a person she was making up. For a while they were separate, Actual Samir and Thought Samir, and when she saw his face at school she'd be surprised that they weren't the same. After a weekend of thinking about him constantly, she'd see him in math and think Oh, is *that* what you look like.

She'd look at his face like he was an exam question to

be read slowly, analytically. If she missed something, she might make a mistake. It was sexy and grown-up, the band of tiny dark marks above his mouth and the charcoal shadows along his jaw. That facial hair just below the surface seemed like the adult part of him, just barely kept in check. And at the same time he was this gangly boy with a sweet face. Because they had three classes together now, she saw him every day and she was starting to get more used to Actual Samir. Sometimes Actual Samir sat across from her at lunch or hung out a little after school. She wasn't sure whether Actual Samir was as nice as Thought Samir: she didn't know him as well.

Chloe's house was close by, which made it the perfect spot to regroup. Chloe's family had the good kind of chips and a second fridge just for drinks, and when you ate the chips or drank the pop, more appeared later.

Erin did not have self-replenishing chips or a second fridge. Erin lived in an apartment with her dad in a neighbourhood where there was always garbage spread over the grass across the road, being picked at by gulls.

In grade six Erin heard they were having choir auditions across town and she submitted an appointment form online and figured out how to get a bus there after school. She was the only kid at the auditions who didn't come with a parent.

Two weeks later she got the acceptance letter and saw the fees: the rehearsals, the uniform, the music, the travel. Her father said he was sorry. She cried all night for three nights. She left a voicemail after hours. "My plans have changed," she'd said in her eleven-year-old voice, which she made as stiff and businesslike as she could. The choir manager called back the next day and told her not to worry about the money. There were a few scholarships; they would work something out. Erin hadn't said anything about money.

Erin helped with the little kids and the fundraisers; her dad set up the risers or handed out programs. She'd travelled to Europe and South America. The conductor had helped her prepare her audition for music school. Even with a student loan and the two jobs she'd be working in the summer, though, she wasn't sure it would be enough. Her dad was really pushing for medicine. He kept bringing it up. She'd got lucky with choir, he said, but other things weren't going to work out that way. He couldn't understand why someone with her grades wouldn't apply. She was perfectly capable.

When he said this, she could see that he really couldn't understand: he had this exasperated, frustrated look. He was totally baffled at her unreasonable desire not to be a heart surgeon. Why the hell didn't she want to? He'd be happy to be a heart surgeon. Or any kind of doctor. And she knew he would, too: he'd be happy to provide for the two of them without worrying about money, to do work that everyone respected. He would have done whatever it took.

Disease terrified Erin, and she didn't want to *have* to do medicine (or law, which was the other one he sometimes mentioned) just because she and her dad weren't well off. Other people got to choose what they wanted to do. It wasn't fucking fair.

Chloe phoned their mom on the landline and asked if they could borrow her nail polish and if so, where it was, even though Chloe was at that very moment unscrewing the cap and setting it on the table. Becca knocked a carol singer off the piano with her elbow and the little china carol book snapped off the singer's hand and speed-rolled under the radiator like a mouse scurrying to get away. While Becca lay on the floor working her rugby player's fingers into the tiny space under the radiator, trying to grip it, Chloe said "Yes Mom, yeah, okay, not the pink" and reached into a cupboard and pulled out the SuperStick.

Erin plugged in Chloe's phone and filmed Alyssa painting Chloe's nails.

"I don't know why I'm letting you do this to me."

"Because you're a saint, Chloe."

"This is the weirdest cultural thing ever, right, smearing shiny carcinogens on the ends of our fingers. Who decided this was a good idea? And why did anyone believe them? If Martians land here, between that and tap-dancing we've got a lot of explaining to do..."

"Alright Chloe, quit moving."

"Honestly I don't think this is your best nail job ever."

Chloe superstuck the carol singer and Becca replaced her on the piano while Erin filled a bucket with ice in the kitchen sink. The singer in her flounced full-length cream Victorian skirt and petticoats and her cranberry bonnet looked as if she found the songbook suddenly heavier; it dragged away from her and hung off her hand rather than being supported by it. But still she smiled bravely.

Alyssa disappeared upstairs to change. Chloe said, "Can someone look on the glue package to see what you wash that stuff off with, I can't feel the tips of my fingers—guys, no kidding, this feels really creepy...*It doesn't wash off? Shit!!!*"

On the back deck Alyssa in borrowed shorts and T-shirt smiled glamorously into the camera and said "I love you Erinnnn—holy FUUUCK!" as the water crashed over her head and ice cubes bounced back up off the deck.

Erin didn't know what the *I love you* meant exactly, or how seriously she should take it, but it was encouraging. If Erin and Alyssa didn't get anywhere with the dating, then probably Alyssa would get to stay in the friend group and Erin wouldn't, because Alyssa had been there longer. And since these were pretty much Erin's only friends, she'd have no one to talk to. Choir ended with graduation, and it had been her life for the last six years. She would be alone all summer, no one to hang out with in the few hours when she wasn't asleep or working. She would have to deal with every decision on her own, would have no one to ask for input or make her laugh, and this seemed unbearable.

Also, her dad might be mad at her forever for wanting to do music. She was afraid of him being mad, but she was going to stand up to him. But what if he was right: how would she know what was the right thing? Her options weren't going to arrive like cheese at one of the fundraisers she'd helped out with, four or five little wedges, each with a teeny identifying flag stuck in it. There wouldn't be an option whose flag said *Pick me!* If her dad stayed angry, she might have to move out and couch-surf. Also if anything happened to him. He was kind of tired and bad-tempered, but she knew he loved her and he was proud of her. If he got sick. That was the list of possibilities Erin ran through constantly: no friends, no money, no dad. And if all of them happened, she didn't want to think about that. She didn't want to think about any of it.

They tried an ice cube on Chloe's fingers in case the glue was like gum but it wasn't, so they scrubbed them with soap and a nail brush, carefully avoiding the fresh polish, and then Alyssa said they'd have to wait for the skin to regrow.

Chloe wasn't planning to sport coloured fingernails for long, but they'd leave them on for the rest of the day to be a team player. Frivolous bodily decoration was not the sort of thing Chloe went in for, as a rule: they were, apart from the odd catastrophic error in judgment, a focused, on-task sort of person. They needed to be on-task: Chloe's anxiety had nibbled away at school work and grades, and although things had improved, it was basically too late. If you blew your grades in high school, it was all over. You wouldn't get into a good university, and if you didn't get into a good university you wouldn't have a shot at the better internships and co-op placements, and without those you wouldn't get the decent jobs or grad schools. If you're climbing a mountain and you fall off a ledge, you can't just pick yourself up and start again: you're dead. Chloe might already be dead.

Chloe's mom said that was ridiculous, no one cares about your high school marks, but Chloe's mom had gone to school decades earlier in a world that didn't exist any more. Chloe was waiting on a letter that should already have arrived and might still arrive (today? tomorrow?) or might never come, a letter that might be an acceptance letter to the university program they'd applied for. They would forget about the letter that might or might not exist for minutes at a time, maybe even half an hour. But then there was a feeling like their heart was a yo-yo doing a jerky bounce when it hits the bottom of the string and changes direction, and they'd remember: there might be a letter, or there might not. If your career was over before you'd even graduated from high school, you might as well have ridiculous fingernails for a couple of days, because screw it.

THE PARK

THE PARK WAS where everyone would be. Chloe and Becca had basically grown up in that park: it was near the three schools they'd moved through, a stone's throw from their houses. They'd swum in the pool and scootered on the paths, played on the equipment and sprawled on the grass, eating popsicles. Now they were jog-trotting along the sidewalk to the entrance.

"Guys," Erin said, "the Abbey Road thing, on the cross-walk?"

Four boys were taking long strides over the crossing by the park gates, one behind the other. They were looking around uncertainly, and without hearing what they were saying, you could tell they'd started without figuring out who was going to take the picture.

"Dudes," Chloe said quietly. "Duh."

Becca shouted "Jaxon! We'll take yours if you do us!" She ran into the road and grabbed his phone and stepped backwards, almost banging into a small red sportscar. Someone honked as Becca took the shot and Jaxon was heard to mutter Fuck you, but they honked again and it was Becca's cousin waving. Becca and Jaxon traded phones and Chloe ran onto the crosswalk with Alyssa and Erin. By this time someone was honking for real, but Jaxon got the shot and they darted through the black iron gates into the park.

Becca was the normal one; they called her that sometimes among the four of them, Normal Becca, because Becca didn't have Accommodations or a Diagnosis. Becca was easygoing and laughed loudly and often, despite the fact that her brother's illness had crept through the house unscrewing all the lightbulbs; there was a black hole in the house and that place was her brother and the darkness emanated from him and spread until the whole house was full of it, her big brother whom she had adored and who had let her be his little sidekick and read to her from books when he didn't know how to read himself but traced the line of words with his finger and told the story in his own way, sometimes incomprehensibly, with singsongy intonations borrowed from their parents. Sometimes she could tell when he was home by walking in the front door and listening; the silence had a thick, ominous quality when he was there, a sense that something bad had happened or was about to. *Hi!* she'd call out, and bang the door shut to make sure they knew, whoever was there, that she'd come home, and she'd head to her room.

There were groups all over the park: a line of leap-froggers, a human pyramid that wobbled and collapsed, three yellow T-shirts arrayed along a thick branch like Big Bird and his family while a fourth tried to scramble up the trunk. Becca detoured to the tree; she laced her fingers together, bent forward and offered her joined palms to the last yellow-shirted boy. He nodded his thanks, stuck his foot in her stirrup, jumped and grunted and dropped back to the grass in defeat.

"You're Gregor, right? From Chemistry. I'm Becca. We were lab partners that time? You got this, Gregor. That was just for practice: come on!" Gregor was short and round-faced and his cheeks were red with exertion and shame and the day's unexpected warmth. He looked about to say no, but Becca leaned to brace herself against the tree trunk and made another sturdy sling of her hands. She felt Gregor's sneaker again and lifted; she felt his hand shoving her shoulder down. She straightened her knees and Gregor yelped, wriggled and was up.

Becca wiped her palms against her pockets and looked straight ahead to where a boy stood beside a picnic table pulling off a faded burgundy T-shirt and tossing it onto the bench. Another boy climbed on top of the table with a small cooler. The boy on the ground held his arms straight out like the crucified Christ in the Bellini painting they'd seen in art class; he stood rigid in shorts and sneakers as the boy on the picnic table emptied the cooler of ice water over him. Samir yelled and shook himself. He brushed the drops of water off his smooth chest as if they were snowflakes; he crossed his arms over his narrow body, clamped his hands under his armpits and shivered, grinning.

Becca's closest friend on the rugby team was Madison, and Madison had told her what guys like, what they like you to do. Madison had said she, Madison, had done those things for Travis, who played on the boys' team. But although Madison crushed it on the field, she wasn't a hundred per cent reliable off it, and who knew if she was telling the truth or if she even knew what she was talking about. Becca needed to look Samir in the face, in person, and think about what Madison had told her, and see if those were things she could imagine doing. What she felt in that moment would tell her what she needed to know. At least she hoped so. She wasn't exactly sure what it would tell her: if her feelings were normal, maybe, or if she wanted to spend time alone with him. She thought she did.

The week before, she'd been stacking her books at the end of class and when she looked up he was standing by her desk. His dark hair hung down over his forehead but was very short on the sides; he was back-lit by the large class-room windows and the sun shone through the outer edges of his ears, making them a pale, translucent brown, which caused him to look, partly because he was unaware of it, slightly vulnerable and entirely adorable.

"Hey," he'd said. "Want to…. Yeah. I was gonna study after school. For the test. At that coffee place, the new one. If you felt like coming, I could, you know. I could quiz you."

She'd ordered an espresso. She knew what it was, but even so it did look disappointingly small for the price and when she tasted it she wished she'd had the raspberry lemonade he'd ordered. She drank a small sip and tried to enjoy it, but it tasted like maybe you were making cake with melted chocolate chips and you burned them onto the bottom of the pan and three years later your mother found the pan and soaked it in a tiny bit of water, and the water was this coffee.

He was talking about the Boer War, about the past exam questions he'd read on the website and the likelihood of certain topics recurring. Smuts, Kruger, causes, consequences, and she watched his expressive, intelligent face from across the table and nodded. He said Smuts and she tried to look thoughtful and imagined him sitting on a couch in someone's basement, unzipping his jeans. She nodded again at Kruger and said Yeah, a key players question, that might happen. And in her head he sat back on the couch looking maybe a little nervous. She wasn't sure about the next part, if she would want to do it at all. What if it was too weird? Probably you couldn't just stop partway through and say "You know, this isn't how I pictured it" and call it a day. He was saying Principal Causes; he was saying Transvaal. He looked really cute when he was at his most serious—an earnest, mildly perplexed expression, with his dark hair flopped down—he had raised his eyebrows, and his eyes were big and deep brown and sort of shining. He seemed to be seeking some sort of approval but she had missed the question. She said British Imperialism in the sagest possible way, a shot in the dark but it seemed to do the trick. What if what she did wasn't the right thing, would he tell her what to do? She imagined her hand and her mouth and his hips lifting and when he said The Pretoria Convention, what do you think? she said Yes.

Becca wasn't looking for eternal love, she wasn't out to cramp Samir's style. All she really wanted was for him to put his arms around her and rest his face on the top of her head and say I know; I know.

Something rustled and crashed down next to her. The shot was done, Gregor was down.

"Thanks a lot, Becky."

"Next time I need a favour, man, I'm coming for you."

They offered the sign with ERIN written on it to a young woman pushing a baby stroller, and she held it up and stood by Erin for the picture.

Erin had met Alyssa and Chloe in the Wellness Centre at school, where there was support for young women who were pregnant or who needed to look after a baby between classes. There was also peer tutoring and yoga and talks about relaxation. There were plants and lamps and a fish tank. It was the place everyone went who had Accommodations—for depression, eating disorders, anxiety, ADHD, self-harm, borderline personality disorder. Lots of the kids were in private counselling, which Erin's dad couldn't afford. Erin took medication for anxiety and depression. She knew her dad didn't get it. He just wanted her to be happy, he said. Well, news flash: it's not like flipping a switch.

The school would call parents near the end of the year

and say Your child will be recognized at the final assembly; you may wish to attend. Her mom lived out of province, but her dad did wish to attend and he took about a hundred photographs of her standing in a corner of the gym with three medals hanging on fat striped ribbons around her neck and two framed certificates, one of which was the Pythagoras Award, for which she would be flown somewhere in Atlantic Canada to compete in the finals. If she was well enough.

The school counsellor had asked if her dad pressured her to get good grades. No, he didn't; she generated that pressure all by herself. It wasn't something she did on purpose, and if she could stop it she would. And quite apart from that, the whole fucking planet was burning up. I just want you to be happy, he'd say, and meanwhile everyone kept flying off on holidays, idling at drive-thrus, drowning in plastic bags.

Erin hated drive-thrus with a rage that almost levitated her right off the floor; she wanted to do a guerrilla assault on the lineup and spray-paint all the cars, screaming her head off. She'd wear a black ninja outfit and use a spray can like a gun and sprint away afterwards into the gathering dusk to a getaway vehicle. Sometimes when she couldn't sleep she played this scene out in her mind. That baby whale on the news was found with a belly full of eighty-eight pounds of plastic shampoo bottles and tampon applicators; there were sixteen rice sacks and some of the plastic had calcified, it had been inside that baby whale so long. The whale's stomach acid couldn't break down the plastic so it broke down the stomach instead. The point of no return was behind them: soon they would all be baby whales; they were the first generation to be totally fucked, all because the previous one just couldn't fucking be bothered. And everyone just wanted her to be happy.

They asked a man to tie Alyssa's shoe. The first man they saw was old and they didn't want to make him lean over, so they waited until a bendier-looking man turned up. He was friendly. He tied the bow funny, so the loops were parallel to the shoe instead of perpendicular to it. They were supposed to ask someone if they could rub their belly, but no one wanted to ask the nice man that. There were teams all over the park by now, lining up on the slide, jumping off swings, doing cartwheels by the bandstand, pretending to walk other people's dogs. The teams didn't all have the same list of challenges, so sometimes a group seemed to be just clowning around and then someone stood in front of them to take a picture and you realized they were actually doing something deliberate and identifiable. Everything was disparate until the camera came out, and then suddenly you saw the scene framed and the composition made sense. Each photo was proof of a collective sense of purpose, regardless of how inchoate it had appeared; a goal had been met.

Earlier in the year Erin had begun to notice a small smudge of white on Alyssa's knuckles during first period. It was there most mornings and gone by lunchtime. Eventually she'd figured it out. Every day Alyssa brushed her teeth after breakfast and ran out the door almost late for school, swiping the back of her hand over her mouth.

For Erin, this minty mystery smudge summed up something intangible and endearing about Alyssa: there was the fact that she was entirely unaware of it, a kind of innocence, and a breathless haste to get on to the next thing. Erin could love Alyssa just for the smudge. She found herself looking at Alyssa's hand as these thoughts ran through her, and Alyssa saw her looking and took her hand and squeezed it. "Are you having fun?" Alyssa asked. Alyssa was looking at her with this huge smile, waiting for the answer but confident about what it would be.

"Yeah, it's amazing! Are you?"

It was coming to an end now, everything. The last thirteen years of their lives, which had only been a few years longer than that in total. And soon they would be doing different things that would require of them more independence, more responsibility. They felt annoyed that this should even be pointed out to them (which it was, all the time) and entirely capable of managing their own affairs. Some of the adult advice given to them frankly sucked and they'd be better off without it. They were (hello!) old enough to make their own decisions. And on the other hand they had a deep-down awareness that they did have a bit of trouble with some things, and what if they couldn't find a good counsellor in the new place? Chloe and Alyssa hoped to move away. They had both, without discussing it, been looking online at what mental health services were offered at the universities they wanted to go to. The four of them would still be BFFs online, of course, but that wasn't the same as having someone to hang out with, not a replacement for being alone all the time.

Adults were always complaining: millennials blablabla, entitled blabla, can't even make a phone call, blaaaa. They didn't know what it was like to grow up in the first generation that would not live longer than their parents, the generation of people for whom there would be not only no careers but no jobs that lasted long enough for you to graduate from a cubicle to an office with a door and a plant gasping its last sunlight-deprived breath, a generation of workers who would experience significant work-free periods of enforced, anxious, impecunious leisure and would have to repurpose themselves every seven years or so to make themselves credible in a completely new field. (Astrophysics? What the hell!) If they were lucky. For whom housing would take such a massive toothy chomp out of their budget that there would scarcely be room for shampoo bars (yes, bars, unscented ones, because they were actually making an effort, not that anyone was paying attention); for whom the earth was lumbering up to incineration mode with an increasingly rapid gait, an earth that would by the time they got old, if they had that luxury, be so hammered and poisoned and generally abused that their day-to-day lives would be unrecognizable to their parents, the same parents who made excuses for their own lazy-ass refusal to leave the car at home and would be dead and therefore not have to become climate migrants, which was why they didn't give a shit about bringing home giant plastic tubs of lettuce, of which (go look!) there were probably at least two and possibly three getting slimy in the fridge at this very moment. Middle-aged people couldn't get it through their heads that the little things—the aversion to phone calls, the inability to buy stamps—weren't coincidental, were in fact caused by the vast, reeking catastrophes that flopped down on the young like weighted blankets. Very weighted. So weighted they were pinned to the couch. What was the point of mustering the skills for a courteous and efficient phone transaction when up to a hundred *thousand* species went extinct every year and no one knew who was next?

And now they might lose the scavenger hunt.

They had felt all along, secretly, that they might win because...well, they didn't really want to say, but let's face it, they were pretty smart. And because they could plan and prioritize and be imaginative and cooperate. Because they could colour-code and make fast, witty jokes and problem-solve, and collectively they knew almost all the American presidents and the Canadian prime ministers and the capital of Yemen. Because they had a certain deep-seated confidence they weren't even aware of that came from being loved. Because, in spite of everything, they still had hope.

THE LIGHTHOUSE

THE LIGHTHOUSE WAS the last thing. Chloe called their dad to find out which lighthouse was closest and he said What? Lighthouse? Aren't you in school? So Alyssa called her mom, who told her to get in that car and boot it out to Fort Amherst, and by the way there was money taped to the roof of the glove compartment and they could go for ice cream when they were done.

Four teams had attempted an alliance of expedience in the park, as a result of which there had been some intermingling and some accidental wandering off and possibly some beer in a gym bag, and one member of Gregor's yellow-shirted team had come apart from his tribe and was going to squeeze in with them on their way to the lighthouse, so as to be dropped off downtown and reconnect with his fellow yellows. Charlie called "Shotgun!" and they all stopped and looked at him.

"I don't think so, freeloader," Becca said.

"Worth a try," Charlie replied, wedging himself into the back seat. He updated them on some of the events of the day. His group had been chased out of the supermarket for eating dog treats.

"No way," Alyssa said, outraged. "It's *illegal* for people to eat them?" Only, it turned out, if you hadn't paid for them, which Charlie claimed he had but perhaps not everyone did. Apparently, in the pet store downtown the lady had given some away for free. "What did they taste like?"

"That dog treat," Charlie said, "is the *hardest* thing I have ever eaten. In. My. Life. I can't believe I still have teeth." This set Chloe thinking about the lime juice and whether their enamel would be permanently damaged. Charlie said his group had walked through a drive-thru and given an order and been refused service; they'd found a policeman who pretended to arrest him, he wanted that photo for his mom and dad, he hoped they got the cuffs in the shot.

"How's it been for you guys?" Erin asked. "I mean, have you had a good day?"

"Are you kidding?" Charlie said. "It's been awesome."

They parked near the War Memorial and Charlie got some footage of the four of them rolling down the grassy slope from the cenotaph before he passed the phone back to Chloe and jogged off. And then they were trudging back uphill, occasionally charging each other and trying to knock the other person into another downward roll. When they got to the top, instead of making straight for the car, they lay on the ground again, each of them stretched out like a sausage—this was a freebie, a bonus for no good reason, no camera, just squeals and the smell of the grass smushed into your face and the dizzy bumpety feeling of pretending to be a log and realizing how uneven a grassy hill is and feeling a rock or a hump press into your hip or your back and coming to a stop at the bottom, just lying there looking up at the sky and waiting for all the swirling elements of your field of vision to slow down and assemble themselves in the appropriate positions.

They got to Southside Road and turned east. Chloe vaguely remembered coming out this way years ago: the road wound between the harbour on the left, where the dockyards and ships gave way to small boat moorings, and the rock face that rose on the right. Everything seemed new, though; there was new fencing, new gravel everywhere, as if someone had decided gravel was an attractive thing and we should have much more of it. They'd built a little place where you could pull over and sit on a bench, surrounded by gravel. There were pylons and rolls of chain-link and pieces of heavy equipment and detour signs. As they drew closer to the lighthouse, though, the construction eased off and they passed wooden houses shoehorned into the rock. Also built into the rock was the occasional metal door covered in rust, padlocked shut—fairy doors, clearly, leading into the hillside, because who else builds doors to a cliff? "Guys," Chloe said, "see that door? Not you, Alyssa: eyes front. I wish we could go in that door!" Eventually they reached the place where you have to park the car and walk the rest of the way.

They'd slowed down. The sense of urgency had waned. It had been fun, the urgency, but they no longer needed it. The ocean was calm, just some low parallel furrows on the water, looking, Chloe thought, like the ridges where the dining room rug got bunched up. The rock face to their right had patches of shining dark where water trickled audibly out through holes in the hillside. The construction had stopped and that was all they could hear, trickling water and the engine from a boat coming out through the Narrows; it was a whale-watching tour and the passengers were being told over a loudspeaker that there were whales out there today and they should keep a lookout. Then fiddle music replaced the voice. The four of them stopped and watched the passengers with their windbreakers and giant camera lenses scanning the ocean. By the time they reached the lighthouse, the boat was well on its way to Cape Spear.

A man stood on the grass near the cliff that dropped to the water; he was wearing a headset and speaking a language Erin didn't recognize into what looked like a fluffy rabbit on a stand. They tiptoed past him and took the steps down to the lower level, below the small lighthouse and past the ruins of graffitied concrete bunkers from the war, down to where guns had been positioned to defend the harbour entrance. There was still a large semicircular iron band embedded in the ground for swinging the gun around, back when there had been a gun, and the cross in the middle that it had been mounted on. Erin put her arms out and moved one foot in front of the other, walking the iron arc as if it were a tightrope. She wondered if she was a real friend in the friend group or if she was the one they put up with. (They all wondered the same thing, but she didn't know that.) When she got to the end and faced the water, Chloe came over and leaned against her shoulder.

"Hey Erin."

"Hey."

"Looks nice out there."

"Yeah." Chloe was warm against her arm, and they swayed there for a moment and rubbed their head lightly against Erin's shoulder like a pony nuzzling in before they straightened and leaned forward.

"Did you see that?"

"What?"

"The spray there. Wait. It's over there now. I think it's—"

"Guys!" Alyssa called from the steps. "Whales!"

It was a small pod, three or four minkes just outside the harbour.

"They don't look very big," Alyssa said. "Maybe they're baby whales."

"Maybe they're Raphael's relatives!" Becca said. "Chloe, get it on video. Oh, we forgot to get the lighthouse. Selfie with whales! Selfie with lighthouse!"

Chloe pulled out their phone and studied the screen. "Guys, I hate to tell you this but someone won an hour and a half ago."

No one looked particularly disappointed. "Ah shit," Becca said. "Oh well."

"Who won?" Alyssa asked.

"Car Twelve. Do we know anyone in Car Twelve?"

"Nah."

"Look, that one's jumping again." The four of them stood lined up against the railing, watching the whales, which were more or less in a circle and then not, disappearing and popping up again, blowing and flicking their tails up, which looked, Erin thought, a tiny bit like when Alyssa lay on her stomach reading and bent her knees and flapped her feet around in the air. Maybe they were doing something that had an important purpose in nature, but it looked as if they were just taking a break from the everyday chores of sieving food into their mouths and avoiding predators and fishing gear; it looked as if they were just clowning around, having fun, killing time on a sunny day at the beginning of summer.

THE LESSON

THE INSTRUCTOR'S NAME was Philippe. He parked in front of the Airbnb where she was waiting in the porch. He paced the sidewalk, looking furious.

"Where is your vehicle?" he demanded.

Angela said, "I'm picking up my rental tomorrow. I thought we were using your vehicle." *Vehicle* was a word she almost never pronounced—she would normally say *car*. And it was a strange word, with that *h* in a funny place where you don't say it but you sort of leave a space for it: *ve*-[space]-*icle*. But he had said it, so she did too. It sounded formal to her, a term the police might use if they thought you'd caused an accident. A term she might use in an academic paper if she wrote about cars, which she didn't.

He said of course they could use his vehicle, and he opened the passenger door and took a few things off the seat: a Samsung tablet, a small notebook, a clear, triangular plastic case that had held a sandwich. The fact that he needed to clean up made her think that maybe she wasn't supposed to be using his car really, despite what he'd said, or at least that he had not expected it. She didn't know what he'd expected.

She said, "Is this the kind of car where you can control the driving as well?" He replied that it wasn't. She said, "I thought with driving lessons that you would have a set of controls." He said no, was there a problem? "Well," she said. "The problem is that we might die." He stared at her. She wasn't what he had expected.

Yesterday Angela had driven in a September gale to an access point for the walking trail where she would meet her friend for a walk. Cathy texted to say she was running late, so Angela sat in the car and pulled out her phone to check in for her flight. She was going to Toronto for a few days to help Ben move apartments. Ben, Angela's first-born, who meant the world to her. Only now Ben hated her. This was since the booking of the trip, since Angela had said she'd come up and help with the move. In their last conversation, a week earlier, she had heard fury verging on hatred in Ben's voice for the first time ever. Ben had said: You've always been unsupportive. Angela was stunned. What she felt was that for years she had driven herself to meet the needs of this young person, had toiled and bitten her tongue halfway off, felt exhausted and beaten down, and sucked it up and carried on. And also that Ben was her friend, her buddy, her sweet and kind and generous young man, whose company she loved, the one who, if she came home defeated at the end of the day, would immediately open his arms.

And now Ben was consumed with loathing and felt she had never been supportive. It was astonishing to her, that they could have such different perceptions of the same events, the same challenges, the same life.

"I know how to drive," she told Philippe, "I do it at home all the time. But that's not the big city, and I'm not the best driver in the world." She would have liked to point out that she could do some things quite well; this just wasn't one of them. But that would sound silly and defensive. Angela had lived away from Newfoundland, yes, but she hadn't had a car then. She'd been a grad student, a sessional lecturer: she'd had no money for a car. "I don't understand all those bike lanes and who knows what. Those painted diamond things on the road. I need you to show me. You're going to have to save us. I don't know how you can do that without controls."

Philippe looked less furious now; he didn't seem delighted to have met her, but there was also surprise, and that had a mitigating effect. "It will be fine," he said, and he handed her the key. She located the side mirrors, rear-view, handbrake, gearshift.

"I need to be able to go from here to my son's old apartment and to the new apartment. I'm only here until Sunday night, and those are the three places I'll be. So if we could practise them a few times, that's really all I need." Philippe nodded and punched the address of Ben's apartment into his GPS.

Angela's go-to social strategy, especially with strangers, was to try to make them laugh. It felt like a responsibility. It was how she tried to take tension out of a situation, to win people over or make them feel comfortable. It had taken her half a century to learn that trying to make people laugh wasn't always a good thing. Sometimes they didn't want to laugh. Sometimes it was awkward. Often it fell flat and she looked like an idiot. But it had frequently proved a helpful gambit, and within a few minutes she and Philippe were laughing as she drove.

Philippe was originally from Senegal. English was his third language. Angela had been careful not to ask where he was from. He might have been born in Toronto. But she mentioned that she was from St. John's and he volunteered the information. He said Newfoundland was the only province he hadn't been to. She was his third lesson today, although it was only noon; he did a lot of instruction and also had a small snow-clearing business, and sometimes he worked security at Queen's Park. He lived with his mother and four children; one more was away at university. He didn't mention a wife and she didn't ask.

Back in St. John's, she'd been sitting in the empty parking lot near the walking trail, pressing the button that said she would not be taking skis or ammunition on board the plane and hoping the wind would drop before her flight. The branches of the bush in front of the car jiggled and flicked; a nearby tree wagged back and forth. The wind was supposed to have died down, but she could feel the car lifting and dropping beneath her. She clicked to add a checked bag in case Ben needed her to bring things home. She was half expecting Cathy to text again to say it was too dangerous to walk in this wind.

"You live with your mother?" Angela said. "Wow. Does she drive you crazy?"

"No. Why would my mother drive me crazy? She is a good woman." Phillipe thought for a moment. "The children, now...." He laughed again.

Angela hadn't known whether Ben still expected her to come up for the move, but she hadn't wanted to be the one to cancel, and Ben didn't say anything. Michael had a conference on the moving weekend, so she was doing double parent duty. A couple of days earlier she had texted Ben about her arrival time and half expected him to say Mom, are you kidding me, you're not still coming. But Ben had texted back to say that he would be at work and home by suppertime and there wasn't much food in the apartment so maybe they could go somewhere.

Ben was in third year; he'd been sharing an apartment with a couple of other students and it wasn't working out. This last year he'd taken a course in medical ethics. Begun volunteering for a bicycle repair outfit. Become a vegan. Most of the bike repair people were vegans. Sometimes they cooked together on the weekends; sometimes he went along. But he'd always been a quiet kid, not a joiner; he still didn't know many people in the city. He seemed to be doing reasonably well, but it was hard to tell, and Angela didn't want this move to throw him off course.

Ben's interest in organ donation had sparked in high school, when they had a guest speaker at an assembly who had received a liver from a young man who died in a motorcycle crash. It was inexcusable that in this wealthy and supposedly advanced country you had to opt in to the process rather than being a potential donor by default. Thousands of people were suffering needlessly because of the short-sightedness of bureaucrats. In high school, Ben and the other members of the social justice club had written the government, pressing for a change in policy, and received in response a polite and mildly patronizing letter that infuriated them.

Angela was all for organ donation. She had created and laminated her own donor cards years earlier—before Ben knew what an organ was. She'd put a card in her wallet and stuck one on the fridge and made sure the family was aware of her wishes. For *after* she was dead. Or largely dead. And she'd consider it now too, if she had a friend or family member in need. But she wasn't twenty-one.

Two weeks earlier, Ben announced that he was preparing to donate a kidney. He'd had the consult almost a year ago and had been through counselling and a variety of tests and appointments since then, none of which he had mentioned. He was a good candidate to donate, apparently. Angela had realized this might be in the works, at some stage, but not so soon. Not now. Not for years.

She was taken aback. Isn't there a process, she'd asked. Surely they don't encourage people your age to.... What if you end up needing it? What about the health consequences for you? She had trailed off in Ben's hostile silence. Ben's voice sounded cold and hard as marble as he pointed out, quite rightly, that this wasn't a new thought for him. It wasn't his job to manage Angela's ill-informed expectations.

He had researched it thoroughly. He had begun researching it a long time ago and if Angela had been paying attention, this wouldn't be breaking news.

Angela had in fact done some research of her own several months previously and found a lengthy and informative document from a comparable national health service. It suggested that donors were normally older than Ben, that the screening was protracted, and that few candidates were ultimately accepted. So she had let her guard down.

Those protocols, Ben replied contemptuously, were excessive and outdated. They had been replaced. He asked weary questions about the credibility of the sites Angela had used in her research, and Angela refrained from pointing out that she had earned three degrees, which was three more than some people had. What she had read indicated that there was little in the way of conclusive longitudinal research: the jury was out on whether it was safe because there wasn't enough information. Ben said it was clearly safe, and with that in mind, he wanted to donate to a man at the bike shop who had kidney disease. Peter had been running a bike repair program for disadvantaged kids forever, had trained countless volunteers to fix bikes, had refurbished and sold and donated the bikes and got people out of vehicles and pumping pedals, some of them people who wouldn't have been able to afford it. Why would she even want to question that?

Despite the volume of information, the call was brief and terse.

· · · · ·

Angela was not going to do any multilane highways, no merging into major arteries. "I'm terrified of that," she said, "I don't know how. If I have to merge, we will definitely die."

"No problem," Philippe said.

Philippe explained about the bike lanes, the buses, the streetcars. "See, here," he pointed at the intersection ahead, "you can get into the right lane to turn, but not until the solid line turns into a broken line."

"Oh jeez. Okay. Is anything coming? I don't see anything. Can you see, are there any bicycles?"

He smiled. "You're doing fine, go ahead. Don't be nervous!"

. . . . .

Wavering was Angela's specialty. She tried to see the other person's side of things, but this was often hard to accomplish in any profound and genuine way, especially when the other person wasn't there. She needed to imagine Ben was there. She'd pictured her mind rising above her body—the body that sat at her kitchen table—escaping through the top of her own head like a wisp of steam from the kettle, that wisp drifting across the table and solidifying into a body that would sit opposite hers. What feelings would occupy the second body? She hadn't a clue. She strove to be empathetic, but sometimes she just ended up making excuses for people's bad behaviour. What was the difference between an enabler and a decent human being? She had trouble judging where to draw a line. Or she drew it so tentatively that no one knew it was a line and they tramped right over it.

The first phone call, in which Ben had said he might become a donor fairly soon, had left Angela feeling hyper and slightly trembly. She'd been getting ready to go out, to the retirement party for a colleague in Earth Sciences. Angela was on the verge of bailing, but at the last minute she decided to carry on and managed to have a private chat with two friends at the back of the room. Over the next couple of days, she called another friend and met a fourth for coffee. All mothers of young people near Ben's age, people she respected, two of them medical, all exhibiting varying degrees of concern.

Of course Ben was an adult. Of course he would make his own decisions. Presumably, they know what they're doing, one reassured her—they wouldn't have let him get this far otherwise. But everyone agreed Angela should encourage delay. She could suggest that some time for reflection was a good idea. No one felt that would be intrusive or unreasonable. But they weren't twenty-one, and they wouldn't be standing by, holding out a Scotch when she hung up the phone.

• • • • •

They drove to and from the three locations until she felt she was getting the hang of it. The old apartment wasn't that far from the new one, and she'd chosen an Airbnb quite close to the old one. There was lots of time left in the lesson: she'd had to book a two-hour slot. They were touring around the neighbourhood, passing a sign for IKEA, when she got distracted and felt she had lost her bearings: were they headed north or east?

"Which way is IKEA?" she asked.

"It's that way," he said, pointing.

· · · · ·

When you are a parent, you have to decide when to speak and when to keep your mouth shut. Angela kept her mouth shut far more often than Ben realized.

She would ask if he might wait before making an irreversible decision. She texted Ben, asking him to call when it was convenient. The first call had caught her by surprise; this one she prepared for carefully. What's the harm in giving it a little time, she would ask. That's all she was suggesting, time.

Ben had been determined to move away for university. Some terms were better than others, but she thought he was okay. He was living his life. He was moving on, doing well in his courses. She dared to hope he might be okay now, grown-up, finished with all that. And now the kidney: maybe he would never forgive her, but she felt morally compelled to try.

Ben was walking; Angela could hear a rhythmic crunch of leaves under his quick-moving, angry feet. A car horn, a bus engine. It was easy to hear these things during the holes in the conversation. As his tone grew angrier, she kept hers deliberately quiet. "How long do you think I should wait, Mom?" Ben had asked. "Till I'm twenty-five?" This was clearly not intended as a question: it was a statement of disgust. Twenty-five sounded good to Angela. Thirty would be good. A six-month delay was better than nothing. But for Ben, being twenty-five might as well mean being wrapped in cloths and entombed in a pyramid on the Giza Plateau. Angela and her ilk were a bunch of old fuddy-duddies, incapable of grasping what was true and pressing and vital in the present moment. And while they twittered and fussed, Peter was getting sicker.

• • • • •

When Philippe returned her to the Airbnb, she would have a couple of hours to prepare herself for meeting Ben. This thought filled her with exhaustion. She'd woken at three thirty to catch the early flight and by evening would be unequal to discussion about anything more complicated than supper. Even that could be a minefield. She would acquiesce in everything. They could have vegan sea urchins for all she cared. What she dreaded was the moment Ben walked towards her with a face like a patio stone.

Philippe continued to direct her for several minutes and then they were taking a turn that followed a curving concrete barrier.

"Oh my god. Oh my god, this is an on-ramp. Oh my GOD! You told me I wouldn't have to merge, you promised!"

"Relax, it is fine, you are a good driver. Go now. Faster: gogogo. Go!"

But her nerve failed at the last minute—she was afraid to slip into the lane: she'd be pulling right out into someone's car, there wasn't room, everything was going so fast, all these little coloured blobs whipping past in a line, like a conveyor belt of horrifically accelerated Smarties. She started to brake in terror and the driver behind them honked furiously.

"GO!" Philippe said.

She didn't know what happened; she might have closed her eyes at the last second. And then they were in the lane and moving forward with the other cars.

"I told you I didn't want to do this."

"You said IKEA."

"I asked where it was! I didn't say I wanted to go there. I don't know how to merge."

"You have to trust that they will make a space for you."

. . . . .

After the walk on the trail, Cathy wanted to give her some soup; she had made a batch, and some rolls, which was why she was late; it had been simmering while they walked. That way Angela wouldn't have to cook supper and pack at the same time. So she stopped at Cathy's place on the way home, following her through the front door. Cathy called a hello down the basement stairs.

"Say hi to Angela."

Adam appeared at the bottom step. How could he have grown so tall? He was bigger every time she saw him; his head looked as if it might graze the basement ceiling. She remembered him small and fair, wearing only a diaper, perfect rosebud mouth, sitting on grass and reaching fat fingers out to touch individual green blades, touching and then retreating and then touching again, as if he couldn't decide whether he liked the feeling or not.

"Hi Angela." He leapt up the first few stairs two at a time and then ran the rest: THUNK. THUNK. THUNK. Stompa-stompa-stompa-stompa-stomp. The never-ending legs pumping, the hair on them, the shiny basketball shorts, the low grunt just before the door slammed: *Loveyamom.*

· · · · ·

They turned around in the IKEA parking lot and took a different route back to the Airbnb, one that followed quieter roads. Neither of them said much on the way back, but there was no animosity; it was as if they had both come through an ordeal—tired, muddied, but alive and grateful. He got out of the car and swung the door shut. She hadn't been sure of the right way to part, but in the end they had to hug: it seemed the only appropriate conclusion. She told him if he came to Newfoundland she would show him around, and he said he would like to bring his mother to meet her. Even though they knew these things were unlikely, they also knew they both meant them in that moment.

Inside the Airbnb, Angela climbed the stairs slowly, holding the banister. She unlocked the door, pushed off her shoes, and lay on her back on the bed. She would be calm. This choice wasn't hers to make. It was entirely possible that she should be making the donation herself, but she was not ready for that just now. At least they didn't need to talk about it any more. She had done her best, and her best had not gone well.

At one point in the second call, a week earlier, she'd

heard a change in Ben's voice, a momentary break from the fury, like a patch of slush on the frozen surface of a pond in February. "I hoped," Ben had said quietly, "you would think it was important because it's important to me. I hoped that would be enough." Angela had stepped onto the slush and dropped into icy water.

Dealing with adult children was baffling. Even the word *child* wasn't clear: when do you stop being someone's child? Ben would always be her son, although he wasn't a child anymore. And as he shifted from child to adult, she remained his parent. She had spent almost twenty years learning to show him how to do things, and now she needed to learn not to show him, that he would show himself. It was a bewildering type of training.

Sometimes it all seemed like too much work—maybe the problem wasn't dealing with children so much as interacting with other human beings. At night she imagined a cave in Scotland. She'd never been to Scotland, but it seemed like the sort of place that would have a remote, craggy cave where she would hang a heavy blanket over the opening and light a fire under a conveniently located air shaft. There would be internet in the cave, of course, so she could work, and every now and then she would venture out for supplies, which would line the rock ledges, like in the Famous Five books. She would do her work and go for walks and gather wood, and there would be no one to remind her of all the times she'd forgotten to use her indicator or neglected to let someone go when she could easily have hung back and waved them on, when she'd slammed on the brakes at the last minute for a pedestrian whom she startled when she just meant to let them cross. No reminders everywhere of all the many and various errors of her ways. Sometimes she fell asleep imagining herself pulling back the blanket and entering the cave. Angela lay on her bed in the Airbnb and closed her eyes, pictured herself tossing some sticks on the fire and sitting cross-legged beside it, at peace in its orange glow.

FOURTEEN STEPS

1. THERE ARE FOURTEEN steps to the next floor; that's how I taught the children to count. The teacher wondered why they all came to kindergarten knowing how to count to fourteen and no further. I go up slowly these days. Sometimes I stop and have a bit of a rest. That cardiologist wanted me to move to somewhere on one level. I think she meant a home, but she didn't like to say so. She said, "Mrs. Norris, think of it this way: your heart has a certain amount of gas in it, and you can use that gas however you like, but there are no refills." She stood up to get a blood pressure cuff and she was fussing with the fabric of her skirt. She pinched it between her fingers—it was a nice skirt, navy and white stripes—and tugged upwards and then did the same on the other side, until she saw me looking. Her undies were sliding down, I could tell. She said, "If you want to keep going up and down those stairs, it's up to you, but is that

really how you want to burn your gas?" She looked about eleven and I was going to say I'd toss a match in my tank if I felt like it and for god's sake why didn't she just pull them up properly and be done with it. But she was quite sweet so I kept my mouth shut. She didn't have that look they get sometimes, the *I am smiling patiently and making things loud and simple for you because you're VERY OLD* look. I know that look. Sometimes it's not a look, more a tone of voice. Just wait till you're ninety-two, I thought: you'll see. If you're lucky.

2. I think I'll stop just for a minute when I get halfway, to catch my breath. I'm quite fit, considering, and my mind is certainly still good. Better than ever, in fact. I've been learning German on that iPad, just little bits at a time, it's wonderful. I'd always had this idea that I wanted to read Rilke in the original. Just a few poems, but I wanted to really understand them, every word, and how the sentences work. That's what I thought, and then I read some in translation and I realized Rilke isn't my cup of tea. He was a bit of a disappointment, frankly. I'm going to carry on and learn the German anyway, though. I like to finish a job once I've started it.

The grandchildren are always saying Nan, you're still sharp as a tack. As if that were something to marvel at. Poor old Harold wasn't stupid, but he wasn't sharp as a tack, not towards the end, when they had him in that corridor where you had to ring a buzzer to be let in and out, and a nurse would come and unlock the door because they didn't want the patients wandering. Those nurses always did their hair and makeup nicely. Some of them were lovely. I remember one who always had dark hair pulled back tight in a low bun and brownish lipstick, a round face with a sharp little cleft in the middle of her top lip. She was very good to us. A nice nurse can make all the difference.

I'd go in mid-morning and sometimes he was white as a ghost, this skinny old man with the pale blue sheets and the white thermal blanket all twisted up around his legs, and he was picking at the bedding; I couldn't tell if he was trying to untangle it or if he'd tangled it up. I loved those hospital blankets, soft cotton, with a pattern of tiny squares that were holes keeping the heat in.

I'd say "Hello, love, it's me, Eileen," and he'd say, "Thank god you're here, my ride didn't come. You'll have to take me to the hangar." And I'd say, "What ride is that?" And he'd shake his head and say, "This whole thing is such a mess." He'd say, "They called the office—engine trouble. Not the main airport: this one's hush-hush. I told them, I said, I don't know how quickly we can get the parts, but they're sending a car. Anyway, I went to wait for the car but they must have got lost so I came back here and took my clothes off."

"All right," I'd tell him. "I'll see what we can do. Maybe I can call them."

They'd have an IV in, and his arm was so thin the tubing looked big. There was a bag of yellowy brown pee hanging off the end of the bed, in clear plastic like a freezer bag. I'd move it to the other side in case someone came to visit, no need for that to be the first thing they saw when they walked in the room. Not many people were coming towards the end, though: what was the point? There was a woman down the hall always shouting *Hellooooo? I need to go to the bathroooooommmmm! Helloooo???* She kept it up all day. She couldn't have needed to go to the bathroom that often, and most of them had catheters.

3. Poor old Harold, what a way to go. He'd have hated it if he'd known. It's not dignified. I've told them—I've told Catherine—they have nice big windows on that ward. If I get to that stage, if I'm waiting for my chauffeur to show up, bring me over to the window to show me the car. Open it up and give me a good shove. I'll be thanking you from the other side.

4. These stairs seem awfully steep today. I'll just sit for a minute.

I collapsed at the top once. Harold called the ambulance. I'd slipped the night before, in front of the house, put my hands out to stop myself. It was icy. Broke both my wrists. I had casts on my two hands and it hurt like crazy. I had to watch my fingers to see if they started turning blue. One day in the waiting room at the hospital I had a chat with a nice lady wearing one of those boots, a sort of boot cast, and she said "It doesn't feel good, I keep telling them, and my toes have been black for days, I'm afraid of what the doctor's going to say when he sees them." And I thought My god, I'd be afraid too, if my toes were black. Actually, it frightened me, that did. I started getting up in the night and going to the bathroom to look at my fingers and make sure they weren't getting darker. If you look at something long enough, it starts to change. A few times I got Harold up; he was half-asleep and thought I was off my head, but he didn't complain. He'd say, They look okay to me. Standing there in the glare of the bathroom at three in the morning in his grey striped pyjamas, his eyes half closed, dark hair sticking out in all directions. He looked like a confused prisoner, and I'd shove my hand in his face and say Look! Look properly!

He was a patient man, Harold. He'd hold my cast and lift one arm to shield his eyes from the light strip on the ceiling, and he'd turn it gently and have a good look, and then he'd do the other one. Then he'd say You're all right, now come on back to bed. He'd pull the blankets up to our noses and hum into my ear for a few seconds and fall right back to sleep.

I'd fallen at the top of the stairs because when I slipped on the ice I didn't think I'd broken my wrists; I thought they were just sprained, so I carried on to bed. And in the morning I hadn't slept and I suppose I was in pain, and Harold said he turned his back for a second and whump, I went down. Good thing I didn't go right down the stairs; I wouldn't have made it. He called the ambulance then, and they took me to the hospital and that's when they put the casts on. For six weeks I had those casts, from my finger joints to my elbows. I couldn't lift a glass of water. I drank from a straw. One day when Harold was leaving for work I went to the toilet and the door banged shut in a draft and I had to wait there for nine hours until he came home.

I couldn't turn the doorknob. After a few hours I piled the towels in the bath and had a rest.

5. Harold came to England as a mechanic during the war, and that was how I met him. A small, dark-haired man with a wiry body. He repaired aircraft engines. Or any engines. He could fix anything, Harold: he just needed a few tools wrapped in a cloth, and a little tin of oil. He was on a few days' leave when I met him, and then we spent time together whenever we could. When the war was over he came for me and we sailed away together. My mother wore a blue dress and new blue shoes and she waved goodbye from the pier. We were crying and waving. I was twenty, and I never saw her again.

6. When my knee gets stiff, I have to get both feet on one step before I can go to the next one. Today the knee's not bad, though—it's this damn heart hopping around. I could call Catherine but I don't want to bother her—she's always so busy, that girl. I've told her: you work too hard, it's not doing you any good. She's lost her figure. It's the stress. I told her those children are big enough and ugly enough to look after themselves, she should take things easier. She doesn't listen, of course. Always had a mind of her own. She's good as gold, though, checks up on me: chats, lunches. I told her there's no need to go out for lunch, I can make us a sandwich. She took me for afternoon tea at the museum café, with the three-tiered serving plate full of little scones and cakes and sandwiches. That was nice. You can look over the rooftops at the ships coming in to

port while you put a dollop of cream on your scone. She stops in if she's in the neighbourhood.

Cath was the one I spent most time with, of the grandchildren, when she was small. She was special, the first grandchild. She loved to come and spend the night and do puzzles. She liked things a certain way: the toast cut in triangles and put in the toast rack at breakfast, and god help you if you couldn't find her favourite egg cozy. A sweet, funny little thing, flicking her plaits back over her shoulders and asking such serious questions.

Her mother, Barbie, was still a baby herself. She did try for a few years, but there were more and more sleepovers at our place and by the time Cath went to kindergarten, she was living here, in her mum's old room. We still had three at home then, almost grown, so Cath had plenty of company. Barbie went to Ontario with a boyfriend for a bit and came back from time to time. It got to be less and less often.

She was broken-hearted after that idiot left her, poor Cath. Took her a while to get back on her feet after that. He didn't know his own luck, that man. I'd half a mind to call him and tell him myself, but she'd never have forgiven me. I hope he knows now.

7. I thought about leaving Harold once. I fell in love with a friend. It was that stage in your life when the children are gone and you're not sure what the rest of your life is going to be, what it's going to be for. We had Cath, but Barbie had said she was coming back for her, to take her away. I suppose I was heartbroken about that too.

You assume when a couple has been married forever, that must be a good thing. But people get bored. They take each other for granted. I took Harold for granted sometimes. Raymond was an old friend of Harold's who'd never really settled down: he travelled a lot for work, so he didn't really have a home, just a flat. He'd been all over the world, and not just for a weekend: he had his favourite coffee shop in Cairo, a hut where he stayed in Thailand and, I think, a little girl in Tasmania. We saw him quite often when he was here: he'd turn up on the weekend and help Harold pull siding off the back of the house or bang away at the pipes in the basement; they'd have a beer and he'd stay for supper. He was dashing, Raymond was, he had a certain something, he made a woman feel special. He wore a moustache, and he'd twist one end of it when he was thinking. They don't go in for moustaches much these days, but I've always liked a man who could wear a moustache. You're looking good, Eileen, he'd say, not in an offhand way but with those big dark eyes fixed straight on mine, and he'd have a bit of a smile in the corner of his mouth, and that look went right through you and your insides felt naked and excited.

One night we went to a party. It was midsummer and there were wild roses everywhere, pink and white, my god the smell of those roses, as if a beautiful woman had slapped you. I'd gone outside to have a cigarette. I smoked occasionally in those days, at a party—imagine! Ray followed me out. He had that moustache and hair down to his shoulders; the men all looked like that then. If you saw the photos now you'd laugh, but not if you saw Ray; it suited him. We talked and he lit my cigarette, and the way he looked at me: I thought he was asking me to move away with him. Everything we said seemed to have its own meaning but also another meaning, as if the conversation were happening on two parallel train tracks headed in the same direction. You might say *Those trees look pretty*, and on the other track it might mean *I want to go behind those trees with you*. We understood both tracks of the conversation, but we only said one out loud. I thought so, anyway. He was telling me about a trip he had coming up; he was going to be working in Hamburg for a month or two. He talked about the area where he would be renting rooms; I'd like it, he said, lots of pastries and art. He said he'd stayed there before and the rooms were quite spacious; there was a balcony. I finished my cigarette and went inside and I was planning it all in my head, what clothes I would take, what to leave behind. He hadn't said anything concrete, but I was quite certain. I couldn't think of anything else. We didn't see him for a week or more, and I thought he was just making arrangements. And the next time he came by, everything was just as usual. There was no sense that he was sending me secret messages, no second train. He was just as charming as ever, but no more. And I realized I'd made a mistake. Or he'd got cold feet. I cried for a year. Poor old Harold didn't know what to make of it: I had to tell him, eventually. I told him some of it. I tried not to let him know the thrill of it.

8. I wish I had that phone. I'd call Catherine now. I'm going to sit down for a bit. It's a shame you can't lie down on

stairs. I don't need an ambulance or anything. If I called her, I might not even mention it. Unless she asked how I was. And then I'd tell her my heart feels like a can in a paint shaker, all vibrations and heavy liquid sloshing too fast.

Hazel will probably call tomorrow, and if she doesn't get an answer, she'll wonder.

9. I don't particularly want to die right this minute, on the steps, in my dressing gown. I'd like to be at the top or the bottom. I suppose the bottom; it'll be easier for them to carry me out. But I'm over halfway up now. Maybe I'll perk up and get dressed. The annoying thing about getting older is that you can't do things you used to do perfectly well. Why wouldn't you be able to do them, when you've done them hundreds of times? It's so frustrating, feeling incompetent. It's probably frustrating for the people you have to ask for help, as well. They've got other things to be getting on with, they've got their own families. Four children— Barbara, Malcolm, Robert, and Sophie—and one more stillborn. That nearly did me in, a full day of labour for a baby we knew wasn't alive. We named her, but I don't say the name. All of them moved away, except Malcolm. Barbie, the eldest: that was touch and go. There was something wrong with the pregnancy. They said I could miscarry at any minute, right up until the end. I kept bleeding, big clots; they told me I had to look at each one to see if it was my baby. But Barbie was determined; she hung in. The midwives took care of you back then, they were very good. And you stayed in for a week—they didn't want you going home

and cooking a meal a few hours after you'd had a baby the way they do now, doing push-ups and exercises for your whatsit. In those days you were entitled to a bit of a break.

Six grandchildren. Catherine's the one I call the most, of course. Sometimes she sends one of the kids over. Morgan's coming today or tomorrow. And that Adam is a sweet boy. He sorted out the iPad when I clicked the wrong thing on Facebook. Deirdre had posted something about missing her father, who'd passed away. And I meant to click on the little picture with the sad face, but they're small and I hit the laughing one by mistake. It took me a minute to realize what I'd done and I was horrified. I clicked everything in sight trying to make it go away. What would Deirdre think if she saw I was laughing when she'd said she still missed him every single day and the angels were lucky to have him for company? I kept trying to fix it. Adam couldn't get here soon enough. I don't know what he did—at first he seemed to think it was funny, but he could see I was upset and then he went serious and somehow he turned the laughing face into a sad one. Thank goodness. He tried to make it sound as if it wasn't my fault; he said the program was twitchy, but I knew. I didn't open Facebook for a month after that, but I like seeing what everyone's doing. I wonder what Cath's doing just now.

10. From where I'm sitting, I can see between the spindles of the banister to the ceramic tile around the fireplace. I love those tiles, the deep green and the shiny glaze. There's not a single room with a level floor. It drove Harold to

distraction, but I love it all, the brickwork in the chimney and the trim around the doors. The rooms are all slightly different shapes, just like the children who grew up in them, and I sometimes think they have traces of each other, that the rooms have hints of the people and the people have somehow been shaped by the rooms. I know that sounds silly. When I think of Barbie, I think of the blue that was the colour of her bedroom walls. I'm not usually fanciful, but I do have a sort of feeling about that. Some people just aren't cut out for motherhood. Barbie couldn't cope. We had to repaint it when she moved away: yellow was better for Catherine.

Harold and I painted and papered all the rooms together; we made a good team. He was better than I was with the fussy bits. I wanted it done properly, but I didn't have the patience. When Harold took apart a piece of machinery, he laid everything out carefully so there wouldn't be a single nut missing at the end. I'd have slapped them down and had things roll away and jammed them back together and the plane would've plopped down out of the sky. He could tell when I was getting bored and sloppy; he'd say How about a cup of tea? and I'd be grateful to stretch my legs and go and do something different and let him get on with it.

Cath tried to steer me towards a condo, she took me to a couple of open houses. Those places have no life to them. It would be like living in a showroom. *Hello, here I am on page seven of* Safe and Convenient Living For Seniors *magazine, opening the microwave and smiling.* No thanks.

I feel as if I can stand up now. I need to get that phone.

I'll call Cath and see what she says. I'll tell her she'd better not let Morgan come.

11. I used to be so afraid of the children tearing down these steps. Whenever we heard thudding that went too quickly, Harold or I would shout *NorunningontheSTAAAAAAIRS!* It got to be a bit of a catchphrase. Long after the children were grown and gone, Harold would hear me hurrying down and call out: *Eileen—norunningontheSTAAAAAIRS!* Well, I'm not running anywhere today.

He took it hard when the children moved out. He'd have had them all living with us forever. He'd complain about them, about their ways and how much it cost to feed them and how little they did to help out (they weren't bad, better than some). He'd shake his head and give that exasperated sigh. But it was all for form's sake: he adored them from the moment they were born. When I was having Barbie and we didn't know what to expect, they told him to go home to bed and come back in the morning, but he was having none of that. He sat in a chair in the hall, folded his arms over his chest, stuck his legs out in front of him, and went to sleep. He told me later that one of us needed to be rested, in case anything happened. And when they let him in eventually and gave him the baby to hold, that was it. Barbie had a little head of black hair just like Harold's and she looked all red and wrinkled and squished from the delivery. She was wrapped in a pale pink blanket, and Harold held her as if someone had just passed him a Ming vase and said Hang onto that for a minute, would you? He bent his head to study the baby. I remember that as if it was yesterday. I didn't know what sort of a father he'd be; he hadn't been around children much. I wasn't sure he'd like them. But his face was full of love. And fifteen or twenty years later, at the dinner table, one or other of them would be talking, telling some story about what had happened during the day, and Harold would go quiet, just watching, and he had the same look on his face. Sometimes he'd glance over at me then and raise an eyebrow as if to say *They're all right, aren't they? They turned out all right.* And I'd nod. Because mostly they had.

12. We had a good run, Harold and I. Ups and downs, of course. No parent wants to bury a child. And Harold felt responsible because Malcolm had always been so much like him, wanted to go to work with him, messed around in the hangar. He grew up loving planes. Bush pilot is a dangerous job. Anything can happen out there. Your vertical and your horizontal can get mixed up. They think that's what happened, that he flew into the ice on the lake thinking it was snow up ahead. But they didn't really know, and it doesn't make any difference now. I remember when Harold told me—there was something not right about his face, as if he'd disassembled it and it was the one thing he couldn't quite put together properly.

Malcolm's room was painted white, and that is how I make myself think of him, flying into something fluffy and light and disappearing into it—no impact, as if he just kept flying, kept going and ended up in a different place entirely.

He's out there somewhere, not able to get back but living a good life, one I can't imagine, having a sandwich and a glass of beer maybe, on the other side of a soft, white curtain. It was hard to keep going after Malcolm. Cath was a great comfort then. Having to get her up and off to junior high and pack her lunch and go to the parent meetings. It made life seem normal. It wasn't normal, but you could pretend.

There are times, too, in a marriage—well, the way I was brought up, you didn't talk about that. You didn't walk away because the other person was driving you mad or you'd had enough of him and you were desperate for a change. You got on with it and hoped it would get better, and usually it did. And I was lucky: Harold was a good man.

There were plenty of fun things. We'd make plans. There was a plan for everything, and when the children were little I realized that for them, the plan was as exciting as the actual thing. You could decide every single thing you'd take on a picnic, every sandwich and cookie, and which colour cup for who, and one of them would make a long list in careful printing, and they'd go and look for the grey camping blanket with the red and white stripes at each end. If it rained on the day, it didn't seem to matter all that much: the picnic had already happened in their minds, or we'd have it in the living room and think of another plan.

Harold and I planned things too: saving for a fridge or a car or a little holiday. Sometimes we went out on the weekend, to dances or cocktail parties. He was quite a good dancer. It's hard to imagine now—he's been gone almost ten years, and he wasn't dancing for a long time before that. But we'd stay up half the night sometimes. It makes me tired just thinking about it now. I do feel so tired.

13. Harold was a singer. It could be Vera Lynn or "Oats and Beans and Barley Grow." He liked *My Fair Lady* and he liked Puccini. He sang along with the kitchen radio in the morning, making toast for the kids. (One butter, one butter and jam, one just jam but not strawberry, one with strawberry jam—he didn't mind doing separate orders.) He sang the children to sleep. He didn't read music, but he only had to hear it on the radio once or twice, he had that kind of memory. If I was upset or worried at night, he'd sing softly to me in bed. He'd lie there on his back, and I'd press myself into his side. I needed to be touching him all along my body; it made me feel safe. He'd put an arm around me and turn his chin so he was singing into the hair on top of my head. He had to be quiet or someone would wake up: a silhouette would appear in the doorway with a teddy dangling from it, and then the silhouette would come closer and lift the corner of the blankets and wriggle in, all bony elbows and knees and little frozen feet.

Whenever things have been hard, whenever I've felt overwhelmed, I've sat and closed my eyes and remembered that, how warm his arm was, that low vibration of his voice in my hair. It was my armour; I felt nothing could touch me then. I still feel that way.

14. I don't think I can stand up, but I'm okay to crawl. I'm going to crawl to the bed and get that phone. I've left it a bit late for Cathy; I think I'd better try the hospital after all.

I'll be all right if I can get to the phone. It's only a few feet to the bed. I can see the pink roses.

I just need to pull myself up on the bed. I'm sure the phone is there. I think I can get up. Good lord, it's ringing. Someone's calling me. Hello? Hello? Is that you, Harold? Just a minute.

DATING

KIMBERLEY NO LONGER had a husband. Not since she'd come back two days ahead of schedule from a visit with her parents and decided to surprise Kev by showing up at their place around the bay with a nice bottle of wine and some brie and crackers. He was surprised. When she pulled over she saw another car behind his in the grassy parking space. She closed her door quietly and walked around the side of the house. It was evening on a Sunday in late September, with the sun pushing sideways across the meadow, against the warm clapboard. She padded along on the grass towards the open window where she could hear them, the thumping and the noises, until she yelled "Fuck you Kevin Whalen, and the cow you rode in on! Get your stuff out of the house in town tomorrow or it's going to the dump." The noises stopped. There wasn't a sound for a while, and then a tentative voice: *Kimmy?*

That was the last of Kevin, and Kimberley wasn't the type to be single, it wasn't for her, so she was trying a few things out, she did not plan to wallow in a wake of misery left by that tool, she was going to go out and have a time for herself. If only she knew where a time might be had. The right sort of time. In the winter she'd gone to some Over Thirty evenings. She was in fact Over Forty now, but there seemed to be a lack of middle ground; there was Over Thirty and Over Fifty-Five. The most senior members of Over Thirty could be the parents of the youngest ones, which was kind of a weird vibe, and the bowling was embarrassing. She was so useless at bowling that she often mixed it up in her head with curling—that long, narrow alley you have to send something down and hope it does the right thing at the end. There was a nature walk, Zzzzzzz. Not that there's anything wrong with nature, but in March in Pippy Park it was basically walking with your poles and ice cleats on a skidoo-flattened path, trying not to let one leg sink down into the snow—it was always one, as if a Great White had chomped on her boot and pulled her towards the centre of the earth for the simple pleasure of making her lopsided. That guy John kept turning up beside her, the one with the watery eyes, whose protruding lower lip was always glistening. She felt bad for him: his wife had died a year and a half ago, he said. But bad was all she felt.

She'd had one date, if you could call it that. Back in February, friends of her parents had set her up with their nephew Carl. The friends had invited Kimberley, her parents, and Carl over for dinner. Let's not even think about that evening.

She'd tried the dance, where there were about seven guys and thirty to forty women, most of them younger than her, where she might have had more drinks than advisable, and even that wasn't enough to improve the evening. Then one of the girls at the firm said she should try online. At first she didn't want to, because one of the few advantages of living in a town where everyone knows everyone is that you can find out pretty fast if a guy's done anything unpleasant, whereas in the ether you don't know what you're dealing with. Okay, the winter had plodded on interminably, but spring had seemed like the right time, the time for budding romance, which surely would happen without the intervention of the internet.

She started walking to the office as soon as the snow melted. It took half an hour, but she had room in her schedule. On the way she passed a house with a composter in the front yard. One day the lid was off, and a strip of banana peel hung over the edge like the arm of someone trying to climb out. Every day she saw a pair of socks two blocks away, flattened into the salt and slush near the sidewalk. Burgundy socks with grey stars; they looked nice. She was half-tempted to take them home and wash them. A week later there was only one sock. That was worse. And one day nothing.

Who abandons a pair of socks? Do your feet feel hot while you're walking up from downtown one night, and do you then take off your socks and put your shoes back on and leave the socks behind?

She tried not to see symbolism in these objects—the

banana, the sock—but she couldn't help herself. Was she the banana, trying to escape from something, or was Kevin the banana, and he'd succeeded? Was she one odd sock, destined to be abandoned and eventually to disappear altogether? The hell with that.

One of the first things Kimberley saw on Chummy.com was a profile with a picture of her cousin Jeff, one that gave his name as Frank and said he was thirty-four. Jeff was the same age as Kimberley. She was just about to text him and say Someone's using your picture on Chummy, and they made you eight years younger, lol...but then it occurred to her that maybe Frank *was* Jeff. Really? Jeff was happily—as far as she knew—married. The second thing she saw was a profile picture of a guy lying on his back in a mountain meadow. He was side-on, his head and feet out of the frame. In the background, a chain of mountains. In the foreground, wildflowers and another little mountain peak under his khaki walking shorts. Ew.

Kimberley dreamed she had a lump below her armpit, on her side, near her breast. A bit smaller than a golf ball, and hard. How could she not have noticed it before? What she felt in the dream was not fear or sadness. She felt resignation. Bad things were going to happen; here was another one. She knew what kind of road she was headed down, the tests, the treatments, the side effects. When she woke up, she felt where the lump had been and it wasn't there. But she didn't feel particularly relieved. Some other bad thing could be lurking just around the next bend. She needed to get her shit together and enjoy her life. It's just that she felt her life would be easier to enjoy with someone else in it.

You're supposed to craft your profile carefully so you attract the people you're most likely to get along with. Kimberley had struggled with the descriptive line and read a bunch of other people's. What was whirlyball? She thought Froyo was a typo for Frodo. She couldn't think of a good movie quote that a million other people hadn't already used. What was the point of saying *fries > quinoa*? Anyway, she didn't mind quinoa. Also, you had to say whether you were interested in BBWs or not. Kimberley looked up BBWs and discovered it meant larger women, but there was no corresponding question about larger men, so apparently you liked them by default. You weren't supposed to say *fun* because that meant you were just looking for sex, although Kimberley actually would like some fun, any kind of fun. Swimming in a pond could be fun. She'd settled on *Safe adventures, good-natured companion*. It was no more meaningless than any of the other slogans. Anyway, she'd read that most people examined your profile while they were sitting on the toilet. How gross was that. What were all those people doing, taking their phones to the toilet? It seemed pointless to agonize about a few words someone might scroll past while they were reaching for the roll of paper. But she got her cousin Laura to have a look at her profile as soon as it went live, to make sure there wasn't anything terrible in there that she wouldn't know about.

Profile after profile slid by of women looking perky, sturdy, sexy, sporty, slutty, stoned—mostly cheerful and pleasant-looking people she wouldn't mind getting to know. She was starting to think *That one looks like she'd be fun to have a drink with* when she remembered why she was there and wondered where all the guys were. She'd clicked the wrong button in the settings.

Immediately discounted: anyone whose picture was sideways, plus the ones whose heads were unnaturally elongated because the photo was stretched. If they couldn't figure out how to upload an image, she wasn't signing up to be tech support. And there were so many, so very many, whose profile said Looking for: Casual Dating. Even Kimberley knew what that meant. BryanJay had added *If things go well, we'll see, could lead to something more*. Hedging your bets there, BryanJay, or just stringing them along? You mean if a girl is reaaaaaally lucky, you might let her hang around a while? Kimberley looked for a Dislike button.

Kimberley had been surprised by the things she missed when Kevin left. He was never much of a help around the house, but he had done some things fairly regularly, like laundry. She didn't love how he did it, but he did it, and now on top of everything else she had to do the goddam laundry. She had thought it would be nice to be alone in the evenings with the electric fire and quiet music in the background, but by July it was too warm for a fire and she scarcely noticed the music; she found herself turning on the TV, which was not how she wanted to spend her time.

Getting nervous about her first Chummy date, or thinking about how it might go, were indulgences Kimberley didn't allow herself. She'd clean herself up a bit and get in there and do whatever people did on dates in bars. She was determined to find something about her date interesting. It was finally warm enough that all she needed was a light dress and sandals. She chose sleeveless blue cotton with tiny pink flowers and a necklace of blue stones she'd bought at a fundraiser for a musician who had been ill. Her mother called as she was leaving, which delayed her a bit, and then she couldn't find her keys. Kimberley would be a few minutes late, which was fine, according to one of the articles she had read, which said that guys are supposed to be on time, but a woman can show up five to fifteen minutes late and the guy isn't supposed to give her any flak. Kimberley dismissed her first thought—that this seemed unfair—because it was perfect for her. She ran downhill to Duckworth, turned down the steps and stood for a second outside the heavy wooden door that could have been the entrance to a mediaeval castle. She rolled her shoulders and took a breath.

Kimberley strode in and ordered a drink, scanning the tables for anyone resembling Patrick, 43, *Looking for a serious relationship—Open minded, thoughtful, active.*

Patrick, 43's head wasn't stretched, but it was wide, and so was his neck; they were about the same width, and when he saw her, he bent that head in a pointed gesture of checking his phone so she would know she was late. He obviously hadn't got the memo about how she didn't have to be a hundred per cent on time and he wasn't supposed to be a dick about it. Read the fine print, Patrick, 43. He had a beer and a glass of white wine in front of him. He looked at the Corona in her hand as if it had said aloud *Hey Patrick, 43, you sure do have a wide neck!*

"I thought you liked white wine."

"Hi Patrick! Nice to meet you. I do, but I felt like a beer."

"Oh. That's okay. You can have it after, I guess." He pushed the glass over to her side of the table.

"Sorry, I didn't know you'd bought me a drink."

"Yeah."

Kimberley set her beer down, pulled out a chair, and sat opposite Patrick, smiling at him.

"So," she said, "what did you get up to today?"

"Not much," Patrick, 43 said. His eyes flicked up and Kimberley saw six or eight men coming in the door, heading for them like a column of loud, burly ants.

"Hey there, my man! Not late, are we? 'Scuse me honey, just gonna bring over a few chairs there, okay?" They dragged another table over and arranged themselves in a row next to Patrick, 43, adjusting the angle of their chairs for the big screen. Kimberley was alone facing the line of fans like a candidate being interviewed for a spot on the team, but they were all looking over her head at the game.

She didn't stick around for the wine.

· · · · ·

Almost a year after what Kimberley had come to think of as Brie and Crackers Night, the divorce was finally imminent. Kimberley was getting ready to move out of her rented condo and buy her own house, a place Kevvy baby had never set foot in, and that was only one of the nice things about it. The kitchen walls were buttercup yellow, the trim was white, and the whole place felt sunny inside and out. She had to buy a few things, one of which was a new dishwasher. When she walked into the deserted store on a Friday night, the washers and dryers in their neat intersecting rows looked like abandoned houses in an appliance village where all the people had fled. The first salesman she saw had said Hi Sweetie and she'd wanted to say Hi Dickwad in return but she exercised restraint. She looked at the dishwashers and said, "I'll want someone to deliver it and disconnect the old one and take it away and hook up the new one, will they do that?" He said they wouldn't do that. Because of insurance, liability, something or other, they couldn't do the connecting or the disconnecting. But dishwashers weren't that tricky—she could do it herself.

She fixed him in her sights. "I appreciate your confidence," she said, which was untrue. "But you don't know if I can do that. Anyway, I don't want to do it. I want someone else to do it."

He had wide cheeks with tiny blood vessels tangled like spaghettini, and he looked mildly athletic, neither young nor old but somewhere in between.

"There's not a lot to it," he said.

"Have you ever done it?"

He showed her to the dishwasher neighbourhood and disappeared while she looked around, returning a few minutes later.

"I just watched a YouTube video," he said. "There's actually a bit more to it than I thought."

"But you said I could do it." She was annoyed enough to rub it in.

"Yeah, but in the video it looks a bit more complicated."

Kimberley scrutinized him and wondered if he was single, if he was active on a dating site, how to avoid running into him there.

The day after the appliance village, she went to a furniture outlet where a businesslike woman named Tammy showed her the dishwashers and said she would need to arrange for someone to unhook the old one and hook up the new one, because the delivery men wouldn't do that. Probably not the sort of thing you want to take on yourself, Tammy said: dishwashers can be complicated. Tammy looked hardly old enough to own a dishwasher, and yet she wore a quiet authority like a classic suit. She provided a card with the name of a guy who would do the necessary.

"We're having customer appreciation days," she said, "there's a table by the door. Have a sandwich, fill out a ballot for the draw. There are cookies."

Kimberley ate a triangular ham sandwich while Tammy prepared the paperwork for the delivery in a month's time. She loved ham sandwiches, and the triangular ones always tasted better. At twenty to nine that evening she was getting ready to go out when the phone rang.

"This is Tammy," said the voice. She wasn't late, not yet, but she needed to leave soon because guess what, it was Saturday night and Kimberley had a date, oh yeah, so take that, Universe of Doom: this just might be the guy who would be nice to her, the one she'd have a laugh with, who would look at her and smile because he thought she was funny and a good person, who would appreciate her better qualities. She didn't want to be late in case Sean turned out to be that guy, and she was standing there with her hair wet from the shower and one leg of her good jeans on and the phone wedged in her neck as she wriggled her foot into the other leg. She had no idea who Tammy was. "The ballot you filled out today? You won. You won a convertible."

There was a brief silence, very brief, it lasted maybe a second, in which she dropped the jeans and thought about guys who drove convertibles. They were usually guys. She didn't like them; they always looked rich and smug, every one of them, the shoulder-length flowy white hair and the tan, she couldn't stand that look. The ostentation. They filled her with disgust. She could sell the convertible, they were worth a fortune, how much were they worth? She could furnish her new house with that kind of money. In the same second she knew that for the first time in her life she wanted a convertible, she wanted to drive along Water Street on a warm summer afternoon with giant sunglasses and the wind in her hair—she'd have to grow it out a little—no way was she selling that goddam car, however wasteful it was, she would keep it, she'd drive it whenever she felt like it. If she looked rich and smug, so be it. So much the better.

"A convertible sofa," Tammy said. "The store's closed, but I wanted to call and tell you the good news."

· · · · ·

She nearly crashed into the building super on her way down to the lobby.

"Oh, sorry, Doug—"

"Kimberley, wait a sec." Doug propped open a door leading from the stairwell to a storage room and gestured into it.

"I can't stop, I'm—"

"Rory. This is Kimberley, in 3C. Rory's gonna be taking over from me here while we're in Calgary." Doug and his wife were expecting their first grandchild and would soon be heading west for a couple of months. A man emerged from the storage room. Floppy brown hair, a long-sleeved grey waffle shirt, faded jeans, warm smile. He looked down at his hands, one of which held a rat trap (empty). He rubbed his other palm vigorously against his thigh for a long time and then offered his hand to Kimberley.

"You're lucky to have Doug," he said. "Good man. I'll do my best." A hint of Scots, maybe. Kimberley shook his hand quickly.

"Hate to be rude, guys, but I'm late!" She flew out the door and jogged downhill and west, rubbing the flat of her hand hard over her jacket a few times.

After Patrick, 43, Kimberley had given up. Not entirely— she wasn't a quitter—but she'd spent a weekend in a cabin on a lake with some of the girls from work, which they did every year, had a golf lesson, visited her parents in Gander. She was thinking about taking a photography class. The summer wasn't a writeoff. But she'd been having a few chats with Sean. Sean sounded nice, and he liked photography too. They arranged to meet downtown for a coffee. He said he was working until eight but he could meet her at nine at Java Live on Water Street west. She managed to be on time, but Java Live was almost empty. She messaged him after fifteen minutes. *Hi Sean, just wondering if you got held up.*

He wrote back quickly: *I'm here at the coffee shop.*

So am I, she tapped, *there's one woman here and a couple of teenagers.*

Must be some misunderstanding, he replied. *Anyway, I had a long day, let's try another time.*

Asshole, she thought about writing, but didn't bother. It had got dark in the time she was in the coffee shop, and you could feel September in the distance like little sharp teeth carried on the breeze; she pulled on her jacket and left.

As the door tinkled closed, a truck started across the street and began to move slowly in the direction she had taken. She didn't pay much attention and walked briskly, which was the way she always walked. She'd thought about safety before, in an offhand way. She wasn't about to go to a stranger's house or do anything really stupid like that. But when she looked over her shoulder some time later and saw the same headlights still creeping along in the darkness just across the road, at exactly her pace, Kimberley felt the base of her throat tighten. She slowed as she approached George Street and then ducked suddenly up the one-way and sprinted. She ran home along a crooked course of side streets, fumbled with her keys at the entrance to the building, cursing, but the door swung suddenly open.

"Oh, Rory, geez, thanks." She leaned back against the

door and pushed, making sure it clicked shut. Rory was standing in the lobby next to an open electrical panel, holding a drill.

"Hey Kimberley. Everything all right?"

"Yeah, fine. Well. Would you mind just sticking your head out there and seeing if there's a truck in the street? I'm pretty sure there isn't. I am sure. But if you wouldn't mind..."

Rory frowned and set the drill down on the floor in a corner. He opened the door and stepped outside, looking slowly up and down the street. "There's no one out there," he said, closing the door firmly. "Are you sure you're okay? Do you want me to walk you upstairs?"

"Oh no, thanks, I'm just being foolish, it's nothing." Inside the condo she put the chain on the door for the first time since she'd moved in.

There were countless articles about how to bolster your chances, how to improve the quality of your profile so it generated better matches. You could answer pages of questions about yourself that might help narrow things down. On good days, Kimberley felt confident that if she kept tweaking her profile until it was just right, she would find someone who was also just right. But how did the site know who would be a match, who would click—literally and figuratively?

Do you have a pet, the site wanted to know. Cat, Dog, Bird, or Other. *Bird?* Kimberley knew one person who had a bird. One. But Bird was its own option. What about all the hamsters and guinea pigs out there, the rabbits and fish, iguanas, ferrets? The axolotls? What did they say about you?

Do you have any pets? SteveM asked. She used a diversionary tactic to avoid answering the question because she didn't know what the right answer was.

Would she seem more appealing if she had a bird? The fact that she didn't happen to have a bird didn't mean she wasn't the sort of person who would like a bird, whatever sort of person that was. Maybe she'd like a bird. She might like one of those sweary parrots.

Maybe she should get a bird and then she could click Bird and it would be true. She could say a few things about herself that could be true, only they weren't at the moment. She could proceed to make them true, and then she would be the person her profile accurately described, some other person who was more likely to get a date than she was. It would be the new, curated Kimberley, whom, incidentally, she had called Megan. (You weren't supposed to use your own name, obvs.) Maybe Megan liked ziplining. Kimberley was terrified of ziplining; she was afraid of heights. Under Goals, she wrote: *Conquer my fear of ziplining.* Kimberley opened a new tab and booked herself in for ziplining the following Saturday afternoon. There was a Labour Day special. She had the whole week to get psyched up. An hour later, a message slid in from Gerard42: *Hey Megan, why are you afraid of ziplining?* If he couldn't figure that out for himself, she wasn't squandering her breath on him. And then SteveM: *Hi Megan, I like your profile. Ziplining's not bad once you get started—just try not to think about it too much before you go.*

The girls at the office thought she was being too cautious and really, cautious wasn't Kimberley's personality. The idea of falling from a great height scared her shitless, that was all. If she thought about it, which mostly she didn't. They had lunch in the boardroom together every day. Sharon was looking forward to retiring, Donna's thirty-five-year-old son was back living with her again, Bronwen was wondering if she should move to Fort Mac to be with her girlfriend. They all felt Kimberley would find someone soon and that the cable above the treetops would not snap at all and definitely not on Saturday afternoon. But of course they couldn't know for sure.

On Wednesday night Kimberley went shopping for a good quality mattress, one that was in stock and wouldn't take six weeks to arrive from the mainland, because the house was closing in four. SteveM had recommended the store in a message. He'd bought furniture there before and they were trustworthy and had their own warranty. The man in the store was scrutinizing his clipboard, which seemed to hold mysterious mattress information, like which ones were in Grand Falls and which ones were in a warehouse outside Toronto and which ones might be going on sale. He was saying "There are a few factors to consider when you're looking at buying a mattress. There's how often it will be used, is it for an adult or a child. A big man is going to need something different from a twelve-year-old." He looked at her. "This is for an adult?" Yes, she said. "For...would that be for, um, daily use?" He made this sound somehow illicit, as if going to bed at night were a gateway to something unmentionable. He dropped his eyes back down to the clipboard and scribbled something as she said yes again. He cleared his throat. "And, this is for...for yourself?" Was he wondering why she was buying a bed now, at this stage in her life? Or did she have *Almost Divorced* stamped across her face? She watched him watching her as she nodded; she felt the heat rising up her neck to her cheeks.

She sat on beds that felt like concrete with a layer of fluff on top, beds she sank into like a coin into a fountain, beds that were more comfortable than anything she'd ever slept on. "It's no good just sitting," he said, "you need to get right on there. Put your feet up, you have to feel how your weight is distributed." She was Goldilocks, on her back, shielding her eyes from the track lighting on the showroom ceiling. She followed the directions of this man who was talking about her weight and watching her lie down. She turned obediently onto her side, which meant that she was looking straight ahead at a spot between his knee and groin as he stood two feet away. A series of folds extended from his fly towards the pockets of his grey dress pants, like rays beaming out from a happy core. His voice wafted down: "This is our top-of-the-line," he said. "Look how many pocket coils there are for the queen, it's a ratio...what do you think? It's nice and firm, right? Yeah. Yeah, see, you can feel the difference."

When she got back to the condo, Kimberley crossed her legs on the couch and pulled a giant pillow onto her lap. She balanced her laptop on top of it. She was probably doing something wrong. Several somethings. She clicked back into the profiles. One photo caught her eye because it looked as if the man was standing next to a knot of black balloons twisted into some kind of shape. She clicked on his photo and looked more closely. TongueinCheek had uploaded a photo of himself standing next to a woman he'd scribbled over in a thick, shiny marker. You could see bits of her head and arm sticking out at the edges; most of her was obliterated. Classy, Tongue. She heard a little ping and a message dropped into her inbox from Derek *Looking4Love*.

Did all those people really like walks and fancy pasta? Kimberley knew she could never say this, but one of her favourite things was to lie in bed at night in a cold room. The window open an inch or two, everything except her face burrowed under heavy blankets, the air rubbing its clean, outside feeling over her nose and cheeks.

Derek *Looking4Love*'s message was disappointing. *Hey*, he said. Kimberley still had a lot to learn about how these things worked, but she felt fairly sure this was not how they worked well. *Hey?* she wrote back. *Hey? Seriously? Is that the best you can do? No wonder you're still looking for a date.* Then she deleted the last sentence. While she was writing this, BeautyKoll sent her three messages. He said *Hi*, and one minute later he said *Hi* again, and in the same minute he sent a third message saying *Hi*. She didn't bother responding to those. Maybe it would be better if she took the initiative. She scrolled through more photos. One of them looked young enough to be her son, if she'd had kids, which she had never wanted. That was one thing she and Kevin had agreed about. It was weird, seeing this baby face pop up in the profiles selected as matches for her. She clicked on him just to see what he was doing there. Kendrick11 had his arm around the neck of a moose with blood on its mouth. Even if she'd been into him, she drew the line at photos with blood. She drew it before that. Before profile pictures featuring death.

And then one day Kevin called and left a voicemail. He knew the "papers" were "underway," by which he meant their divorce was nearly final. It was over with Marion, though, totally over, and he would like to try counselling. Would she like to try counselling? It was strange, hearing his voice. She listened to the message twice and then deleted it.

She would not like to try counselling. The reason the "papers" were "underway" was that he'd been bonking Maid Marion in Conception Bay North. Kimberley had dragged him to counselling in the past and he had sat there as if it was all beneath him and had the gall to look the counsellor in the eye and say in his most affable way that nothing she did ever irritated him, which was horseshit. He just wanted to make himself look like Mr. Reasonable and Easygoing. There would be no more goddam counselling.

After Sean and the creeping truck, she hadn't been in a rush to try again. It wasn't just the uncertainty; it was the psychological preparation, the monitoring of one's own behaviour. Pants or skirt? What to say and what to leave out? It was managing your own feelings when you got home afterwards. She'd been messaging back and forth with three or four guys, and Greg, 48 sounded okay. He'd asked if she'd meet him for a coffee, and she decided to go for it. In the daytime. Greg, 48 was punctual and agreeable; they talked about movies, places they'd like to visit, and how they spent their time outside work. He was an administrator at the trades college. Gregory Hennessey (Greg, 48 actually *was* a Greg) had blond hair on its way to grey and an average build, stood several inches taller than her. He looked like a regular guy, which was just what Kimberley wanted: not a perfect man, not someone who was never bad-tempered or wrong, but someone who would stand beside her when it counted and be a decent person, who would laugh with her and listen when she was upset, who would be pleased when she got into bed with him at night. Or during the day. Someone who had her back. It didn't seem like a lot to ask. She was more than prepared to give those things right back.

It was strange to be walking along the harbourfront beside him, watching the boats and sneaking the odd glance his way—wondering what was going on in his heart of hearts, what were his thoughts and needs and wants, buried way inside that burgundy North Face jacket—but they got along fine. He was easy to talk to. They talked about work. She told him about accounting, about dealing with small business owners and how they were often incredible at doing whatever their thing was—designing wedding dresses that belonged in an art gallery, finding ways to use fish skin to treat burns, guiding kayakers who'd never hefted a paddle along a jagged coastline—and yet they couldn't deal with a column of expenses. Not that they couldn't add them up: the spreadsheet did that for them. They didn't even get that far. They couldn't document expenses or explain what they were or remember in which year they had occurred, which they would know if they had kept the receipts. One of her new clients was a famous artist, invited to give workshops all over the world, who hadn't filed her taxes for five years. "Look," Kimberley had said, "I know, all that categorizing, it's overwhelming when you get behind. It can be hard to know where to start. Just give it to me, hand it all over. Give me the box of receipts, the cash register slips, it doesn't matter if everything is all just tossed in there. Give me everything you've got; I'll figure it out somehow."

The artist had stared at her, an unnerving, penetrating, blue-eyed gaze. "You don't understand," she'd said. "There is no box."

The artist was a challenge, but mostly Kimberley got them sorted out, organized the spreadsheets, generated the reports. Somehow, she made things balance out. And Greg knew a fair bit about that because he oversaw some substantial budgets at the college, they had satellite campuses overseas—regular appointments and short-term hires, matching the enrolment figures that shuffled up or down with the staff who were available and capable of teaching certain areas. Some years everyone wanted to be a pastry chef: you could end up with a rolling pin shortage and paramedicine instructors twiddling their thumbs if you weren't careful. They exaggerated their stories a little bit and laughed, and when the wind picked up he took her arm and they walked linked up like that for a while, trying it out.

Three times a week Anisha appeared on her yoga mat on Kimberley's laptop. Anisha lived about fifteen hundred miles away; it was their way of keeping in touch. Kimberley did three planks, each shorter than the previous one. A few stretches, a few crunches. Lying on the floor was a good way to notice a faint line on the ceiling that could signal a leak, or dust balls like teeny haystacks under the couch.

Kimberley lay on her back holding a cloth strap with a loop at the end into which she inserted her foot, which she then raised towards the ceiling, causing an elongated pinching sensation along the back of her straight leg. Anisha would say, Tell them this. No, you don't want to say that. You can email. Or: Don't email, call. Anisha was usually right. Anisha would empathize, and, on a bad day, check in again later to see how things were. She would send emojis blowing kisses that always made Kimberley feel a bit better. Another day it would be the opposite. She'd say to Anisha: I want a text by four p.m. saying that you've at least spent ten minutes at it; I want to know what your prioritized list of three tasks is.

Today what Anisha said was: Well, are you going for it, or are you just dipping your toe in? You need to decide what you want.

On Saturday morning Greg sent her a note inviting her for dinner. He'd roast a chicken: did she like chicken? She drew a long breath. She was going for it. He sent his address. She said she would see him at six, unless she fell out of her harness and got impaled on a spruce.

She reread the instructions for ziplining. You were advised to wear a rain jacket if it was raining. (Who did they write these instructions for?) Heels and flip-flops were discouraged. She wore leggings and layers, with a jacket that would cut the wind. Rory was trimming the hedge in the small front garden. He had a tarp down for the clippings.

"I'm going ziplining," she announced to his back. She said it so that she couldn't turn around and go back inside and put on some more coffee. If she didn't leave now she would miss the van that took a group into the wilderness, and she felt a distinct lack of sadness at that thought. Rory's clippers paused and he turned his head.

"Really? Ziplining." He sounded astonished, as if he'd never heard of it. "Wow. Good for you, then! Have fun."

"Thanks!" She gave him a little wave and crossed the road to the parking lot.

They gave her a helmet and gloves. The gloves felt stiff and fibrous, but when she climbed the five or six steps to the platform, Kimberley had the urge to stretch her arm out for a falcon. She'd stick out her hand and a speck wheeling in the sky would circle closer. Before long it would alight on her glove, because *alight* is the word you'd use for that. An elegant creature with murderous eyes—who needed a parrot? A falcon would be badass. She would stride off along the hillside, "Kimberley with Falcon" (in case anyone was thinking of turning it into a painting), past the wind-stunted trees and scrubby vegetation, the lichen on ancient rock. A man would step out of the woods farther down the hill, a tall man with curly brown hair and one of those puffy white shirts that guys are always wearing in period dramas. He'd probably have on riding pants. Who knows why. Who cares? Think Mr. Darcy. For that matter, think Chris from Human Resources, if he weren't married, which sadly—although she might have heard they'd split up....

Anyway, Chris Darcy would check her out and see the badass falcon and be totally impressed. They would disappear into the woods together and soon the bird would be flying free.

This was much more pleasant than paying attention to what was about to happen, which could conceivably be the last thing that ever happened, which was why in her head Kimberley was off in the woods with Chris Darcy and not giving the guide her full attention.

"You're going to need to slow yourself down on this run," the guide said. His name was Dylan or Devon or something like that; she hadn't retained it when he introduced himself because she had been wondering if, as she was about to get in the van, she could just *not* get in the van instead. The day seemed as if it would go much better that way. He looked vaguely familiar. The guide had driven the six of them here and led them up the steep hill from the gravel spot by the side of the road where he'd pulled over. He was youngish and fit, he wore a black ballcap from a craft brewery over what appeared to be a shaved head, and those expensive pants where you could rip off the legs if you got too warm. He'd loped up over loose rock like it was a gentle, grassy downward slope. Just when Kimberley thought her heart might explode, the guy behind her had said was there a big rush or something, and the guide stopped to give them a breather. And now he was saying that if they didn't brake, well let's just say they needed to brake on this run. It was a long way to the next platform and people did tend to pick up some speed as they went, so they should use the gloves to slow themselves down: they would grip the cable and squeeze. They should start doing that as soon as they saw the far platform.

"What if you can't, what if you do it wrong or your glove falls off or something?" Kimberley asked. "Can you do it for us, from here?"

"Your glove won't fall off."

That sounded like a no.

The far platform had a huge crash pad attached to the posts, like a mattress standing up on its side, he said. Kimberley could have asked about the coil ratio but she didn't. They would see on approach that the crash pad said SLOW in big letters, to remind them to brake. Kimberley wondered what would happen if you fainted or had a heart attack, but she decided not to wonder that aloud; she didn't want to jinx anything. She wondered how you would see the far platform if your eyes were clamped shut so tight your eyebrows hurt, to make sure you didn't catch a glimpse of the ground waaaaay below through a tiny slit of light you might let in by accident. Because if you didn't see the platform then you might just go whump, and despite the mattress, the guide was making that sound like quite an undesirable outcome.

Kimberley was thinking of saying she'd be happy to wait for them. She'd be happy to wait all morning. She knew where the van was; she would just walk back down the hill and meet everyone there in a couple of hours. She could wait until next week if necessary. She'd build a lean-to in the woods. Or she'd walk the hour's drive back to town. They could take their sweet time.

The guy who had run out of breath on the climb was the first to go. Harness clicked in, one hand on the T-bar, he raised his legs and stuck them straight out in front of him and slid away with a yell of exultation. Kimberley wanted to cry. The only thing worse than going was waiting to go, though, so when the guide asked who was next she said Me! and smiled as if she actually wanted to, as if she thought that barrelling forward at speed from a couple of hundred feet above the ground was a good idea. She was so terror-sick she was starting to feel angry. What the actual fuck did these people think they were doing, running cable this far off the ground? What kind of maniacs signed up for this crap? She hated the guy who had just gone, with his stupid enthusiastic shout. Asshole! She smiled at the guide with a smile so hard she thought her cheek muscles might pop. She hated the guide. Alex, that was it. Fucking sportsy Alex, she hated his guts. It was basically his fault she was here. She wasn't going to be able to brake and she would smash into the crash pad and have to be helicoptered out and her best hope was that she wouldn't make it to the hospital. Second thought: her best hope was that the enthusiastic yeller would do that and then the rest of them would be spared. She was only doing this because of the stupid goddam dating profile and now she didn't care, she didn't want to be the kind of person who ziplined: she wanted to be some other kind of person altogether, one who definitely did not zipline—and she'd changed her mind about dating and about men and she just wanted to be alone forever, on solid ground.

"Okay," Alex said, "legs up."

"Fuck you," she said so quietly no one could hear, and she lifted her legs and sailed into the void.

It didn't get better. She was powering along at the speed of her little blue Hyundai in a school zone, *sans* windshield. The wind was trying to claw the face right off her. And that wasn't the worst of it; she didn't mind if her face got ripped off, in the grand scheme of things.

She saw that there were trees. They probably looked nice. Whatever. There was ocean in the distance, which was fine if you went in for that sort of thing. This is what she discovered by opening her eyes a tiny bit every now and then to see if it was time to brake yet. There was a zingy noise of the T-bar on the cable and she said Shut the fuck up, but it kept zinging. She squeezed the cable with her glove to brake and then she braked some more but she wasn't slowing down a lot, and then she braked again and this happened a few more times until she smacked hard into the vertical mattress and no further braking was necessary.

There were two more runs, but the biggest one, the longest one, the First and Worst, was over. The other two, Alex said, you didn't need to brake for because of the angle; you'd just slow gradually. They were uneventful. They were neither better nor worse. (That was a lie. They were a little better, but Kimberley wasn't ready to admit it yet.) But the thing about the third run, the final line, was that when she stepped onto the platform she felt a tiny bit like the guy breaking the tape in *Chariots of Fire*, which she had seen four times because it was one of Kevin's favourite movies. She did not feel bloody but unbowed. She felt bloody and very bowed, totally bowed, but she had survived, she'd done it, she would never have to do this again. She had tested herself and passed the test. She was now the kind of person who ziplined. Another time she might actually enjoy it. Well, parts of it. Maybe. She wasn't likely to find out.

She liked Alex now. She loved Alex. He had got them all through safely. The others, god knows why, had clearly had fun. Kimberley was the only one who hadn't been able to make the leap from risk to thrill to pleasure, who remained stuck at risk and saw things taking a different course. Yes, she said, as they all climbed into the van, Oh yeah, amazing, oh yes the view, OMG, totally coming back next summer.

She ended up in the front, beside Alex, who looked her over when he swung himself into the driver's seat.

"Doing okay there, Kimberley?" Oh yes she was okay now, and the faster he turned the key, the better she would feel, the distance between herself and the platform expanding with every second, as the ziplines receded into the past: hello, life. Alex pulled up at a stop sign and turned to look at her. "All good?" Did she look weird? What she felt was relieved—not in an exultant way, but in a quiet, lasting way. When they stopped, Alex unloaded everyone else's bag before hers. People high-fived and headed away from the van, waving, and Alex reached in and took out her knapsack. He looked down at it. "You're not, um. You're not on Chummy are you, Kimberley? I mean, I know you're probably not, I'm hardly there myself, just you know, I happened to see something about someone who was going to be trying out the lines. You did great for a first time."

He hesitated.

Kimberley had a sudden flash of insight. Did she want to look over a glass of wine into someone's eyes and remember his nonchalant thumbs-up as he consigned her to oblivion, the harness's nauseating jerks as it advanced over the cable, the zingy whine of the cable like a mosquito the size of a pterodactyl?

"No," she said, "not me. But thanks for everything, Alex!" and she turned and walked away as fast as she reasonably could. She had a date to get ready for.

Greg lived on a quiet residential cul-de-sac near the Village Mall. She took off her shoes in the front porch. He kissed her on the cheek when she arrived, and she handed him a bottle of wine. Beyond the porch was the living room, which became the dining room; she took in burnt orange walls and black leatherette dining room chairs, the comfortable kind with a high, straight, padded back.

"I need a large glass of that," she said. "I was in a harness today, sliding along a cable two hundred feet in the air." Greg looked suitably impressed. She didn't go into a lot of details, and she was glad he didn't insist: her ordeal was now safely in the past, and over dinner she could feel herself unwinding. Greg seemed relaxed too; the chicken was good and the conversation felt more natural every time they talked. After dinner they sat on the living room couch with coffee and he kissed her.

He was warm and his body felt solid and comfortable. He put his arms around her. She liked the feel of his wool sweater, which was dense and slightly scratchy and felt as if several more inches of it could once have protected a real sheep from fierce January storms. She kissed him back. This was already a significant movement from their last date; if the evening had been Google-mapped, the little blue dot would have been advancing rapidly along the squiggly line to the teardrop marker whose pointy little bottom stabbed the ultimate destination. It was enough for her to take in today, which had been long and exposed her to many new vistas already, but she was realizing that he had expectations, that he had spent a chunk of the afternoon cooking the chicken and going out to buy the strawberry pie. It wasn't a trap, it was perfectly reasonable, but he thought that her coming to this burnt orange room for the evening had meant something specific, and she should have anticipated that. Now that his tongue was driving towards her molars, it seemed incredibly naive, but she was realizing she'd just thought she'd see how they both got on, what it was like to have a meal together. She hadn't thought that the latter part of the evening was a foregone conclusion, more that they could see how things went. They had gone fine so far, and now she'd like to go home, and yet it seemed she was too far in for that.

She had erred in communications and strategic planning. She should have built a formula into the cell that stipulated a certain number of walks per dinner, and because she didn't, they had arrived at the equals sign too soon. Which was okay. Her bad. She had led Greg astray, unintentionally, and now she was going to have to go along with it because otherwise he would feel surprised, angry and led on, and honestly she couldn't really blame him. This would be a chalk-it-up-to-experience kind of evening.

They moved to his bedroom. He was rougher than she'd expected; she was about to call a halt when he heaved and groaned. She forced herself to lie still for three minutes as a courtesy, watching digits that glowed green on the alarm clock by the side of the bed.

Kimberley had not thought, as she'd whipped through the sky earlier that day, Oh this isn't so bad. She'd hated every millisecond of it. The worst part wasn't dizziness or nausea or the possibility of death. It was enduring the situation moment by moment. Why had she got herself into that situation? It was entirely her own doing. And when there was still time to extricate herself, she didn't.

She'd thought it would improve as she went along. Things could hardly get worse, surely, after she stepped off a few boards into empty air with little protection other than the fakest of fakey-fake smiles that even what's-his-bake must have seen through. Alex the Outdoorsy. Kimberley had assumed, not unreasonably, that after the first few seconds or minutes or other unspecified units of time, she'd start to feel a little comfortable with the situation. She'd been wrong.

It wasn't a short ride. It went on for frigging ever.

And then the fourth green minute shone out and she was sitting up and twisting her bra on, snatching her underpants up off the carpet.

"Thanks, Megan." Greg sounded muffled. "Hope that

was fine for you. Hey, there's no rush."

On Sunday morning, Kimberley's email notified her of a message from SteveM. They'd been writing periodically, with no talk of coffee or dates or things you had to get ready for or decide about. It felt like how she talked with Anisha, only with a flirty edge. Of course, it was easy enough to sound nice in a message when no one knew if that was your real name or photograph. You could be an axe murderer with a fake profile saying how much you like baby rabbits.

She sent a brief note to SteveM as a courtesy, but her heart wasn't in it. There were a couple more messages from names she didn't recognize and one from Greg, and she would really rather have jumped in a vat of boiling oil than talked with him. She'd have done it willingly, emerging from the pool house onto the outdoor boiling-oil pool deck in a bikini and flip-flops, feeling heat rise from the gloppy yellow surface. She'd watch him pulling up on the other side of the chain-link fence and jumping out of the car, wave cheerily as she plugged her nose, and leap in feet-first. Fortunately, there were other options. She snapped the laptop shut and decided to drive to what would soon be her sweet little house and park outside and look at the garden, make some plans. Maybe she would buy a gardening implement. One of those little fork and mini-spade sets or whatever the hell people needed when they gardened. A pitchfork. A small tractor. Gardening had never interested her in the slightest, so that was about to change right now.

Outside the building she saw Rory sitting on the patch of grass near the steps, legs sprawled out in front of him. He was holding a thermos mug. Beside him, a plastic grocery bag overflowed with weeds. The knees of his jeans were brown.

"Don't you take days off?"

Rory laughed. "I like gardening. This is just me relaxing." He reached behind him and swatted around for a stainless steel bottle. "I made coffee, would you like some? I can run in and get you a mug."

She hesitated. "No thanks," she said. "But I'll sit here with you for a minute?"

"Course," he said. She sat beside him, stretching her legs out and pressing her palms into the grass at her sides. "How was the adventure yesterday?"

She sat up straight. "What do you mean?"

"You were going ziplining."

"Oh, right! God. Well, I think the views were beautiful. I didn't see a lot of them." They chatted about heights and fear and whether being brave meant clicking on the sign-up link or walking out the door with a feeling of dread and still not running back inside again, or opening your eyes when you were whooshing over the treetops wondering if, in case of a fault in the equipment, you would have a heart attack on the way down or crash on the rocks. And whether courage was a term better reserved for more serious matters. She told him about her new house and how she wasn't sure what to do with the garden, which was overgrown. He said he could have a look if she wanted, maybe offer some advice, which was exactly what she had hoped he might possibly say.

"I'm not doing much this morning," he said, flicking his cup so the last few drips flew into the flowerbed. "If you like. Got a few things to take care of this afternoon though. Doug and Ella are coming back on Tuesday, so I need to get this place squared away."

"Oh! You're leaving us. I'm sorry to hear that." And she was sorry—suddenly, shockingly sorry.

"Yeah, my partner was working in Norway for a while, so this was good timing for me. But she'll be back soon, and we'll head on home to Corner Brook." She'd never inquired into Rory's circumstances, where he had come from, any of that. She felt as if she'd just settled in to watch a really good movie and the power had gone out during the opening credits, and it would be out for days, so she would be stuck freezing in the dark, unable to make a cup of tea.

Kimberley had read—some time after she'd signed on—that Chummy was a site people used for grooming, for drugs, for sharing porn, for money laundering and who knew what else. The fake profiles with faces of obscure movie actors or wholesome, smiling, square-jawed farmers in Wisconsin or wherever...lots of them were fake for a reason. But plenty of the people floating around there just wanted the same thing she did: someone to love and be loved by. She didn't know what the numbers were, how the columns balanced out: how many were pedophiles and dealers, how many were just normal folks looking for some-one who might have a bird or like Froyo or hikes or want a bit of a chat while they pulled a frozen pizza out of the oven and cut it into wedges when they got home from work.

Some people said snotty things about dating sites, but let them point to one human being who does not long to be loved, who does not long to look into the face of another and be met with love.

Kimberley might be terrified of heights, but had she not soared through the skies, supported only by a skimpy scrap of cable? She could be brave when she needed to. And now she wondered if all those souls on Chummy (the non-criminal ones, anyway) were not so much lost as brave. They were putting themselves out in the world; they crammed hope in their pockets and set forth, whistling with deliberate nonchalance.

Kimberley blinked. "That's great for you. We're going to miss you around here." Rory stood and offered a hand to help her to her feet, but she scrambled up on her own.

HOUSE

for Karl and Larry

THEY MOVED IN forever ago. The tall one with the dark hair and pleasant, square face does something in government. Something public-facing: he's quite well-known. Used to be in government, anyway—retired last year. The other one's a graphic designer. They bought when you could snap up places around here the way you sweep cookie crumbs into a dustpan. No one was fixing up then. Hardly anyone. Didn't have the money, didn't see the value. If you'd told them real estate would more than triple in value, they'd have laughed. In those days, this block looked like skid row, not a tourism commercial with popsicle houses. It was all rotten boards and sag. Doors with so much paint peeled off them that you couldn't tell what the colour had been. People weren't coming down here—they were sprinting for the burbs in droves. They wanted finished basements with dartboards and wet bars. They wanted built-in closets and the odd electrical outlet, not chimneys that keep exhaling fragments of themselves onto the living room floor. Good riddance.

These two, though: they weren't in it for a do-over and flip. They were aiming for a slow marathon. I'll be honest: I was suspicious from the start. They had to believe—in the project, in themselves, in each other. What were the chances? And they were young, my god. Not the fat cats they are now. Okay, fat is harsh; they look comfortable, let's say. The days of struggle are behind them. That kind of struggle, anyway. If the water boiler dies, it's not a game-changer. They order another one.

So yes, I was of two minds about them at first. I've seen a few bodies come through my front door over the years. It's all very well to have a vision of your future, but can you stay the course? Do you have grit? I can make things difficult when I don't like people. There's so much that can go wrong. Heh. I'd be lying if I said I hadn't enjoyed putting the odd obstacle in someone's path, if they're a pain in the ass. Pry up a loose floorboard and: surprise! But these two, they weren't in a hurry. They got on with it quietly. I didn't notice much change for a while. But one day you see a photo of what you used to look like and think Oh my.

They did the obvious first. Start with the roof, it's the only thing over your head. Then the wiring, so they didn't fry in their bed at night. And over time, the room-by-room. By time, I mean decades. In the summer they were out the back. Stone patio, rhododendron and weigelia, red Adirondacks by the kitchen door.

In the beginning they did a lot of it themselves, and when they couldn't they were on hand watching, doing the grunt work, offering snacks, learning how. These days of course it's not like that; they pick up the phone. They're getting a little long in the tooth for that sort of thing, not that I'd say it within earshot. The tall one's a bit sensitive on that subject.

I've seen them sitting in the living room at night in T-shirts and shorts, each one cross-legged on a yoga mat. Ha! That was enthusiastic but short-lived. There were the days of running, ditto. They still go for walks, though. And there were the parties, the dinner parties, my god the wine bottles, stumbling around turning the lights off when the sky brightened and the last guests left, sweeping the next afternoon around the pink-stockinged leg of one stray who'd slept on the couch, scooping the leg up and slipping it back under the throw.

It hasn't always all been tasteful restoration and floral shrubbery, though. I've seen the tall one sitting head in hands at the kitchen table, talking about work, the words forced out in painful clumps. Talking about hateful statements made calmly, about loathing delivered in a reasonable tone by colleagues. The other one looking sad and worried and pulling a chair up close, leaning in and rubbing up and down between shoulders blades, up and down, side to side, up and down. And I've seen what's come through the mail slot a few times. The neighbours on one side never spoke to them in fourteen years, and then they moved away. What is wrong with people?

The eighties were the worst. The plague years. They kept getting dressed up in dark suits, looking nice but no smiles, and came home holding hands and went quietly to bed. There were lots of those for a while there—lots of friends who didn't come around anymore. Some of them I'll admit I missed too. I'm not nostalgic about people: they come and they go, that's the way of it. But the big funny one, and the one who looked like Marlon Brando. The little one with the oddly shaped ear who looked like a pixie, what a sweetheart. I'm not sentimental—I got used to them, that's all, watching them enjoy their food and tease each other in the living room. You get used to having people around, and then they're not there anymore. They lost most of their friends.

That was a long time ago now, the dark days. They had their own dark days too. One day the shorter one, the graphic designer, was packing some things into cardboard boxes from the liquor store. A bit of spring cleaning, I thought. That evening the boxes were gone and so was the graphic designer.

There were long calls and calls so short that hardly any words came out. The tall one went to bed early, got up late, and didn't do much in between. Visits where they stood on opposite sides of the living room, as if it wasn't big enough for them, as if one had rabies and the other didn't want to get bitten. As if they were making space for a crowd that might arrive in the middle of the rug.

Once, just once, shouting in the backyard at two in the morning. Not shouting exactly. Drunk on frustration and grief and a couple of bottles of the expensive wine saved for a special occasion that was all that was left in the cupboard. For some reason the graphic designer ended up in the backyard, the tall one at the window on the landing. The graphic designer was calling up, lit in sporadic flashes by a wonky motion-detecting light over the back door. He kicked at the dry leaves that had formed swirls under the glass-topped patio table. He wasn't prone to weepiness, but angry sobs interrupted his sentences like commas of misery, a punctuation of rage and the disappointment that came from too many moments of hopeful expectation trodden on.

The opportunity to do the right thing is like a room in which you make a decision, in which you act—you can pull out a frying pan and cook something good for yourself and the person you live with. You can give it a fair effort but still burn it: also acceptable. Or you can amble through the room in a self-absorbed haze and leave through the far door and head upstairs to the thing you feel like getting back to, leaving someone standing alone and hungry by the shiny chrome toaster.

"It's not okay to be oblivious all the time, you know. The way you behave. It's so fucking easy."

"I know." The voice wafted faintly down. "I'm sorry. I know it's not good enough. I'll do better." The hall light was on and his head and shoulders were bowed on the other side of the screen; he was bending down to talk through the bottom half of the window. "Why don't you come back in?"

"You say that, but it only ever lasts two weeks. It doesn't really change." A light came on upstairs in the house next door, the one where the couple lived who dropped their eyes or crossed the road at every encounter. The man had had an injury of some kind in the winter, had left one night in an ambulance and returned a few days later with a cane, the wife helping him up over the snowy steps. The graphic designer had shovelled out the parking space in front of their house and the taller one had made partridgeberry and lemon muffins and left them on the doorstep with a note. The muffins stayed there for two days and then reappeared on their own step, the note opened and stuck back in its envelope.

The tall one was trying to lift the screen, to lean out, but it was stuck. "I'll do whatever you want." The herbs glowed when the outside light kicked in, almost neon green against the surrounding blackness. Mint and thyme, rosemary and sage gleaming in clay-coloured plastic tubs along the edge of the patio stones.

"You always say that! And then you don't." He was weeping now at the duration of it, the prolonged feeling of being undervalued, like a ringing in his ears that never really went away. He knew he needed to choose between two options, one a cataclysm, the other a sustained erosion.

"I didn't realize."

"That's not an excuse, being an idiot! You just can't be bothered." A window slid open next door and he turned towards it. "You two can go fuck yourselves."

When someone looks at the person they've shared every part of their life with and the look says *I have had enough of you; your situation no longer interests me*—not everybody can come back from that. It's not really a lack of caring; it's hurt, an accumulation of wrongs that overlay an otherwise innocuous action.

Three months of that, give or take. And then one day it was toilet paper boxes, arriving in the hall. *Fluffy softness*, it said on the boxes, but they weren't soft with each other yet, not yet. No one was fluffy. Still careful, stiff, polite in a guarded way that had more to do with defending the battlements than raising the portcullis.

It took a while. Lying in bed straight and separate as railway ties. Watching a TV comedy and refusing to laugh because that implied an openness they weren't feeling. But what happens is you accidentally do something nice. If you're a nice person, it's just a reflex. An unplanned nice thing, and the other one is surprised and does something nice back a little later and then the portcullis is wedged up a bit and you maybe cook a good meal on a Friday night and have a drink and watch something you do laugh at, and one day the railway ties are bending towards each other under the blankets and the three months slowly disappear into all the other months and years that surround them.

They knew how to have fun, how to take care of each other, and they still do. Here's how you know: you can tell from the way one brings something to the other one, it's *Would you like a drink, shall I put on some coffee, tea, a glass of wine, what do you feel like? Oh no, you don't want that, do you? Come on, will I make you a...?* It's taking the time to decide what is exactly the right thing for the other person in that moment, as if it were an important decision, as if there were a right answer and finding it required due consideration. It's about consideration. The wedding photos—why they bothered getting married at that point I don't know. But I do understand it, and anyway it's their business. That photo on the patio, framed on my living room mantelpiece, the two of them side by side, looking happy and proud enough to slay you. Each proud of the other. Proud of having deserved each other. Standing there in their matching outfits. So yes, it turns out they had grit. And at the end of the evening it's up the stairs, pyjamas and teeth and some sort of anti-aging night cream for the tall one, sliding in under the new comforter, quiet murmurs and then nothing, and I watch over them till morning.

WORK-IN-PROGRESS

MORGAN GOT UP at noon and borrowed her dad's car for the afternoon. She was going to the Mall to buy him a birthday present and then volunteering on the seniors' walk at the lake.

At the Mall you could buy measuring tapes that said *Work-in-Progress* or *I Am Canadian*—which seemed like a weird thing to announce on a measuring tape. Did other countries have measuring tapes like that? Ones that said *I'm Dutch,* in Dutch? In case you forgot who you were while you figured out whether the new fridge would fit into the space left by the old one? There was a stand of mugs that said *I'd Rather Be* _____ but the only choices left were *Gardening* and *Doing The Crossword,* and her dad didn't like either of those things.

Morgan examined a hard hat with a beer can holder stuck to each side of it. Straws looped out of the holders and over the top of the helmet, ending in a mouthpiece like the one on her brother's gaming headset. Maybe she'd buy it and save it for Adam's birthday. She reached for a T-shirt that said *Well Preserved*, checked the size, and took it to the counter.

Morgan didn't want to be at her dad's anymore. He had his wife and their ten-year-old son, and they didn't shut her out, but it wasn't home. She was thinking about moving back in with her mom and registering for courses in the fall. She didn't really want to go to university, but she didn't really want to keep on working at the restaurant full-time either. Those seemed like the two options.

Morgan paid for the T-shirt and watched the guy wrap it in tissue and tuck it inside a grey paper bag with string handles. She made her way to the escalator. From the food court, you looked down onto treetops crowned not with leaves but with cream-coloured discs made of what looked like stiff felt, discs the size of dinner plates, arranged like the petals of a geranium. She glided down past these oversized flowerheads, then past the giant stalks that looked like real birch trunks. It wasn't clear whether they were meant to be trees or monster flowers or something in between. When Morgan stepped off the escalator on the lower level, she turned to take a closer look.

A grove of four tree-flowers sat in pots on a low wooden platform. Each one rose below the skylight to the full height of the escalator. The platform was painted green and the pots held soil, or fake soil, topped with something that looked a bit like grass. The trunks had the slender, gently curving elegance of birch, and Morgan felt an urgent desire to know whether they were real. No one was looking, so she stepped onto the platform and rubbed the pad of her index finger down the closest trunk. It felt more or less like a tree, but it was hard to tell.

She carried on to the next one, stroked the bark, wrapped her hand around the trunk and squeezed. She wanted to know if it would feel cold, if it was bark glued around a metal pole. The weird thing was, if these were actually trees, how they would turn into flowers on top. Next to the sixth tree she set the grey paper bag with the T-shirt down on the platform and gripped the trunk in both hands and wiggled to see if it would sway; there was some give, but it was stronger than it looked. By then she had decided that they were in some way alive, and the grass seemed more convincing. Maybe there was a big soil tank under the platform.

She followed a path through the grove for a while. She could smell the flowers now, and although they looked like geraniums, the scent was orange hibiscus, which she recognized because it was in the shampoo in the bathroom at her dad's place. The path forked and twisted, and she needed to get the car back, so she turned around. She wasn't entirely sure of the way, but after a while she saw the little grey bag sitting at the foot of a flower-tree, and soon she was picking it up, hopping off the platform, and walking quickly towards the parking lot.

· · · · ·

"So we were in the lunchroom," Laura said, leaning into the trunk of her car and rummaging through a plastic tub. Across the road, blobs of silvery white flickered across the surface of the lake, where the sun brushed over them. Laura pulled out a first-aid kit and a clipboard made of transparent fuchsia plastic. "He was telling me about his new girlfriend, and he said, 'It's funny, I don't usually go in for bigger girls.'"

"Seriously?" Morgan said. She reached for the clipboard.

"Can you imagine me saying: 'I went on a date with a guy but I wasn't into him—because he had a receding hairline JUST LIKE YOURS, PAUL!'" Laura paused for a moment, her face set in furious indignation, but then she burst out laughing.

"Have a clue, Paul." Morgan grinned and tugged a stretchy Volunteer armband until it slipped up over her elbow.

"Really. Maybe I should give up and stick with Barthy: he keeps my feet warm and he never argues." Laura's eyes were dark brown, skilfully ringed with eyeliner. She kept them fixed on you so you felt like the most important thing ever. No wonder all the seniors loved her. "Here comes the bus; do you want to sign them in and I'll get going with the first ones?"

· · · · ·

Morgan was at the back of the pack with Herb, a loose line of walkers snaking slowly before them.

"What's new, Herb?" she said. "How's that grandson?"

"Trouble," Herb said happily. "Trouble on wheels. He's going to be over there feeding the ducks; Melanie's bringing him." She could hear someone behind her talking, maybe on his phone, and then he was passing her and Herb, spitting on the ground, the smell of booze and stale cigarettes trailing behind him.

"Fuck," he said. "You people think your shit don't stink." Morgan was careful to sweep her gaze past rather than looking right at him, a thin man in a knee-length faux-leather coat despite the warm weather. He wasn't having a good day. Morgan cast her eyes instinctively ahead: Sylvia was right in front of them, and a little farther up, Margaret and Noreen, both looking frail.

Sylvia spoke with a ringing Scottish clarity that could be heard for a hundred miles. "We've come to do a walk, and we don't need to hear any language like that." Morgan could have smacked her up the side of her smug face. The man had already passed Sylvia and might have kept on moving with his angry mutterings, but when he heard her, he stopped and looked around to see who had spoken. He resumed walking but backwards, lurching, so he could face them.

"Fucking cunt, judging me," he said. Morgan watched for a knife or a sudden move, poised to shove Sylvia aside if necessary. She was eyeing Herb as well. Herb was tall and capable, but he'd had a few health issues, and Morgan wasn't sure which of them might protect the other.

The man kept stumbling along the path in reverse, glaring at Sylvia, saying "You think you got the right to fucking judge me." His spittle flew in the humid air. "My friend at university with me, she saw her husband shot and then she did that program with four kids and…I'm stunned as me arse and she was fucking amazing. And you feel like you're god's gift."

He wasn't in university now, Morgan figured. Whatever path he'd been on had not served him well. His tone was rising as his body jerked with each step.

"No one's judging you, pal," Morgan said, as calmly and evenly as she could, but ready to lunge all the same. She'd protect Herb—she loved Herb anyway—she would even protect that self-righteous cow Sylvia if she had to, which would be annoying. What a pain in the ass if she had to take a knife for Sylvia, but so be it.

Because she'd spoken, his attention turned to her, and he faltered. "Morgie—that you?"

She curled her fingers tight and nodded, because when she looked at his face she knew immediately who he was. Eddie Dunn, who'd lived on the next street and been a couple of grades ahead of her in school, not that he was there much by the end. Everyone else except her family had stopped calling her Morgie by about grade five. She hadn't seen him for years.

Eddie, who had stolen her new winter hat in grade three and worn it jeeringly, walking in front of her as often as possible. A white tuque with a stripe of red around the band that had turned up in the Lost and Found eventually, the white turned dingy grey. Who'd given her a ride on his brand-new motorcycle when she was fourteen, which was possibly the coolest moment in Morgan's entire life, zipping around the neighbourhood with her arms wrapped around Eddie's waist, glued to the back of his leather jacket.

"Hi Eddie."

"Yeah, hey." Eddie looked as if he might say something else but instead ducked behind some bushes and disappeared, leaving her and Herb to carry on, with Sylvia stomping stolidly forward in front of them.

The path circled the lake, where a child in blue rubber boots was throwing seed at the ducks. The lake ate the toes of his boots. A woman called to him and he turned and smiled. "Have no fear, little Mommy," he said. He saw Herb then, and ran to him, wrapping his arms around Herb's leg.

Aiden inserted himself between Herb and Morgan and reached up for their hands the way small children do, with full confidence that anyone would want to take their hand and swing them forward. Morgan tried to imagine what it would be like to feel that way, to move through life assuming everyone will adore you. She and Herb swung Aiden and he sang Rain, rain, go away, come again and don't come back tomorrow. He said he thought Mommy wanted some Legos for her birthday. Mommy didn't allow cookies before lunch but, he pointed out, lunch was over now.

· · · · ·

In the geranium world, instead of leaving Eddie to beat his angry way through the bushes and seeing him later sitting in the back of a police cruiser, she walked beside him until he had calmed down a bit. They talked about the time the boy down the road, Zachary Maher, had a frog he kept in a bucket in his backyard that he called Hoppy Maher, and when Morgan had run into him years later he had angrily denied that Hoppy had ever existed, even though both Morgan and Eddie remembered him. They recalled the time Eddie's mother had complained to a large food company about some gross thing she had found in a package of crackers and how a delivery man had shown up at the door a few weeks later with two giant bags full of packages of cookies they were never allowed to have because they were expensive and bad for you, and it was cookie heaven at Eddie's house every day after school until all the cookies were gone.

· · · · ·

Morgan was waving goodbye to Herb on the bus when her mom called. She decided to accept it.

"The car battery's dead. Do you think you could pick me up and take me to Nan's later on? I'll only be in there a minute."

"Um," Morgan said.

"She's not answering again. I just want to make sure she's fine."

"I can swing by Nan's in a few minutes. I have to get the car straight back to Dad. It's on the way. "

"What if I get a cab there and you run me home?"

Morgan was enjoying being on the other side of the car argument for once, the person with the keys, the one who had the power to grant the request or not. "Mom, for god's sake, it's fine. I've done it before, I'm sure she lost the phone again. I told her I'd visit today or tomorrow anyway."

Cathy eventually gave in.

"Ask her to call me later, please."

Morgan rang the bell and knocked on the door and bent her knees a little to punch in the code below her great-grandmother's door handle.

"Nan?" Silence. "Nan, it's me, Morg. Just coming in to make sure you're okay." Morgan checked the living room and kitchen. Her great-grandmother would be having a nap. She ran up the stairs because she was already late with the car and her dad had this stupid thing about lateness, like it was some kind of moral failing, not just that life sometimes didn't go according to plan. She was dialling her mom's number on her way up the stairs to tell her everything was fine. "Nan? Sorry to wake you." She pushed open the door to her bedroom with one hand, and when it swung wider, she saw a pale blue dressing gown that had been dropped on the floor by the bed. And then she realized there was a figure underneath it.

This had always been a possibility, even though, since it had never happened before, it hadn't seemed at all likely to Morgan. But she knew how to handle it. She would be calm and clinical. She hung up the call that was still connecting to her mother and dialled 911 instead. She dropped to her knees and touched her great-grandmother's cheek, which, thank god, was warm. She put her phone on speaker. She set it on the floor and lay down so their faces were close.

"You're going to be okay, Nan." To her immense relief,

her great-grandmother's eyelids lifted; her eyes were rolled up high.

"Harold?"

"Hang on, Nan. You're going to be fine."

That is what Morgan would have liked to say; it was what she meant to say and in fact what she thought she had said. She had given key information calmly to the dispatcher, she felt. She had said: early nineties, generally good health, no sign of bleeding, still breathing. That was her sense of the conversation, pretty much. It is what she said in the geranium world. In real life, what she heard someone say was not *You're going to be fine* but, as she moved her mouth closer to the phone, *Oh, this is bad. This is really bad!* She heard a voice sounding neither calm nor clinical. *Nan!* the voice was shouting. *Nan! Can you hear me?*

Morgan stood back to let the paramedics kneel and lean over her great-grandmother and load her gently onto a stretcher. At some point Cathy had slipped in and spoken to one of them quietly while the others slid Nan into the ambulance. She'd shot into the kitchen, opened a cupboard and swept four pill bottles into a sandwich bag, taken them outside. Cathy had leaned into the open window and spoken with the driver for a few moments, nodding, and then stepped decisively away, as if she'd been the one giving the order for them to leave.

Morgan watched her mother. She had seen this before, the Cathy who zipped down the fire pole, snatched the yellow suit and jumped in the cab of the fire truck, slamming the accelerator. That wasn't what she did, but it was how she did it. She was good, Morgan had to hand it to her. She got shit done. And now, with Nan in professional hands, Cathy turned her attention to Morgan.

"I'm really sorry you had to deal with that," she said. And even though they both knew Cathy had done everything she could to prevent this exact situation, even though that fact lay unspoken just beneath the surface of their conversation like a barely submerged reef, even though Morgan had resisted her, which is why it had happened, even though her mother sometimes bugged the living shit out of her, Morgan also knew that her mother meant what she said. She meant it one hundred per cent; the last thing in the world she would have wanted was for Morgan to have this image of the pale blue bathrobe wedged in her brain as if she were in the front row of the movie theatre and the same clip was playing like an ad she couldn't get rid of: the door, the robe, the shape of a person beneath it; the door, the robe, the shape.

"Are you okay?" Cathy asked. Morgan nearly reached a hand out towards her, but she felt awkward, so she just nodded and Cathy said, "All right, then."

Morgan worked a wedding. She and Nathan were serving, Susan and Ahmed in the kitchen. She felt a band of sweat above her upper lip, a damp stripe down the back of her black dress as she slid in and out through the patio doors, past the rose bushes to the tables and chairs set out on the stone terrace and the grass beyond. The couple were two guys who'd been together forever, a big old row house downtown.

Everyone was in the backyard for hors d'œuvre, champagne and cake. She and Nathan worked well together. They rarely needed to speak. She'd bring a stack of napkins when his hands were full and he was busy serving, although he hadn't asked her to, because he'd given her a look with a slightly raised eyebrow, which she knew meant *napkins*, although at another time it might mean something entirely different. As she offered a tray with the last delicate fig and goat's cheese phyllo flower to a guest, he appeared at her elbow with a fresh platter. When she worked with Lydia, they used quick gestures—a hand tilted to the side with the thumb out, as if pouring, meant *I need another bottle*. But with Nathan a look was usually enough. It was a telepathy of convenience.

When Morgan had told her mother who the clients were, Morgan's mom said one of them was a celebrity, well-known for his position in government but also his charity work. And he'd written a book or two. A name everyone Cathy's age would recognize, and lots of others too. After the finger foods and the cake and another round of drinks, he thanked them individually, shaking their hands, and told them they could pack up; he and his husband would take care of the rest.

They stowed the catering gear in the van and unloaded it back at the restaurant, where the crew was cleaning up. The rule was a single drink after work, at half price, and not until every task was complete. After the kitchen floor was gleaming and the mop had been wrung out and stood in a corner, they sat with their drinks and talked about ponds.

They'd propped the front and back doors open to get some air moving. There were differing opinions about the best places to swim. Suddenly the drinks were being tossed back and they were bound for Pippy Park—wait staff, kitchen staff, dish crew, bartender, night manager, a dozen of them crammed into two cars, all elbows and knees, the ones on top trying to distribute their weight evenly over the laps beneath them.

At the end of the cul-de-sac they tumbled out the doors like popcorn and stumbled along the trail in the dark, following jerky blobs of light from a few phones. There was some dispute about where they should turn off the main trail. You had to veer right by a particular bush. But there were bushes everywhere, and it was one in the morning. "It's kind of a low bush," Chef said.

Morgan, Nathan and Ahmed were bringing up the rear. By the time they arrived, the tiny beach was covered in food service workers stripping off. The moon was bright and it reflected off the water. Here were Morgan's colleagues, people who tallied thousands of dollars at the end of the night and did the inventory and knew exactly how to char the herbed salt crust on the outside of a hunk of rib-eye to make it crunchy and not damp or burnt, how to deal with employees who had stolen money from the tip jar or weren't pulling their weight, how to do a million other things more complicated than taking the orders and serving. Morgan was learning, she was getting better, but sometimes she felt like someone who belonged in the kiddie pool and had got tossed in with the grown-ups by mistake.

Here they all were, hopping and lurching towards the water, trying not to tread heavily on rocks, and Nathan hadn't noticed them; he was mostly turned away. She was trying not to stare, trying to look as if she was gazing vaguely elsewhere. And then she realized he *had* seen them, although this barely registered in his expression, just the tiny flicker of an eye. That smallest movement on his face, and his shoulder turning to offer them his back: that was what she loved about Nathan. His decency, his default setting, which was to do the right thing. He was extending them a small gift, which was privacy.

Morgan felt less drawn to the right thing. She sometimes preferred the look of the wrong thing. She occasionally felt an irresistible compulsion to do the wrong thing out of curiosity.

The geranium world wasn't a different place, but one in which the same things happened differently. There, she'd rein herself in a bit. She wouldn't do so many of the things she regretted afterwards.

And then she hauled her dress over her head and ran into the water as if it was the last plane leaving town before the earthquake hit. Morgan was a decent swimmer: she could do a mile in the pool, could hold her breath for a while. Soft, cold pond water smoothed the sweat off her body and tugged away the stickiness, the spills. Everything slid away and sank to the murk on the bottom. She felt cool and free as she moved beneath the surface and opened her eyes in the clear brown water. She pushed her arms out in sweeping circles and allowed her legs to spread wide before snapping them together, leaving behind the shadowy limbs of other swimmers as she drove forward into the heart of the silent pond. There, Morgan wouldn't have to decide whether to go to university, or to wonder whether anyone besides her parents would ever love her, really truly love her, enjoy her company, would they think she was a beautiful person, not in body for god's sake but the whole of her being, would anyone ever think that or was it too much to hope for.

THE LOVE
OLYMPICS

THE DIFFERENCE ISN'T between summer and winter—the difference is that with these Olympics, you compete in everything. You're in the hundred-metre race, but a couple of months later it's beach volleyball. The next day you could be trudging up to the top of the luge run. It's okay, though: the events are spread out. And you've been training for this your whole life.

When you were a baby, you cried and your mother came to the side of the crib and picked you up. You wore the barnyard jammies she'd made you, short-sleeved red flannel with two white buttons between the neck and the shoulder that had required her to learn the buttonhole feature on the sewing machine—chickens and pigs and a cow surrounding your soft body, head turned sideways, a sweaty wisp on your forehead, cheeks getting hotter as your little face scrunched itself up with the effort of crying.

You woke in the night and cried a plaintive *eeh, eeeh, eeaaaaaahhhh,* and your mother jerked awake and propped herself up on one elbow to see the alarm clock. She slung her legs over the side of the bed and pulled a zippered hoodie off a chair and threaded her arms into the sleeves as she moved towards you, stretching her toes apart on the wood floor. She bent and reached down and slid her hands under your body; she raised you carefully and drew you to her and you tucked yourself between her breasts, your head under her chin. She zipped you inside her hoodie like a kangaroo.

You had no idea. When she stood beside your crib and watched you in the dark, when she walked up and down the hall holding you because she was afraid that if she sat down she'd fall asleep and let go of the most important thing that had ever existed...you were in training then and you didn't even know it. You didn't realize your mother was wearing track pants and a whistle on a cord around her neck. You didn't wake up and say: Hey coach. But that's just because you didn't fully wake up. And because you couldn't talk.

Your first romantic relationship? That was basketball. You were learning how to give and to receive, how to work in a team; there was back and forth. You loved, deeply. You played your position, passed the ball. But sometimes you were selfish. You broke some rules when you shouldn't have. Your sense of personal responsibility, which is now if anything excessive, had yet to mature. The ref didn't always call the fouls, but you carry them with you. You didn't know that thirty-five years later you'd still have one of the old balls, that you'd keep it at the back of the closet and every now and then you'd see it and be suffused, drenched in a torrent of feeling. The ball fades away before your eyes and instead you see a face. You wear the fouls still, but mostly what you feel, even now, is love.

Some events you're better at than others. Wrestling is your Achilles heel. In truth, there are quite a few of those: you need more legs to accommodate all the flawed heels. You need to be an Olympic spider. But it's just you, plain old biped with good days and bad days, trying to do your best most of the time. You stride out into the ring, self-conscious in that unflattering singlet-and-shorts bodysuit, and spread your arms, but the woman facing you looks betrayed. She is disappointed in you and has stored up a list of grievances. You face each other, weight shifting from one foot to the other, and you're not sure what she wants; you are both circling warily, but it could all end right here. You would give away the match happily; you would give her anything she wanted: you open your arms for a hug but she goes for the neck and you're both in it then, locked tight, heads together, rolling on the ground, scissoring legs. "I saw you limp out here," she says through clenched teeth. "I know that old trick."

You say, "I have a sore heel." She presses your shoulder down, but you resist and flip and you both roll again. Every time the two of you are matched, the same roles emerge. She, hurt and angry. You, baffled.

"I talked to my friends about you," she grunts. "They agree with me."

She is smaller than you but fierce; there is time left in

the bout and maybe it's not too late. You're so close now, twisting and wrenching in a vigorous embrace, her cheek pressed against yours—anything could happen. You say, "I'm sorry I missed that practice," but she is determined to push you away and she does, and you give in, two shoulders pinned and the ref slaps the mat. You don't fight her again.

Biathlon is a defining event. It's how life goes most of the time. Imagine yourself on cross-country skis, an oval course surrounded by evergreens. Lap after lap, fast and hard through snow-covered spruce and pine, forcing breaths out of your mouth that hang in the cold air through which you are advancing, *huh-huh-huh* in sync with the *shush-shush* of your skis. It's a dance involving your legs and your lungs. You are glad of the freezing air. You'd do it in a T-shirt. Finally you drop, heart pounding, *huh-huh*, kicking off the skis and grabbing the rifle. You need to stop entirely now, to be a still thing, to pause the blood belting through your limbs, steady yourself to shoot. Steady, steady, steady. Fire. Fire. Up and do it again. Come on, you've got this. It's not going to be easy, but you have a heart as big as the world.

ACKNOWLEDGEMENTS

I have read the Acknowledgements section in several books to help me get a sense of how to finesse this tricky sub-genre and they are so witty and generous that I feel doomed to failure from the get-go. Also, I am petrified I will forget someone. If I have forgotten you, please don't take it personally and, if it's any consolation, rest assured that I will remember your contribution one day after this book has gone to the printer's, at 3:36 a.m., and be racked with guilt all night and for many nights to follow.

Many thanks to all former and current staff at Breakwater Books who have had a hand in this collection. Three cheers for publishers that care enough about writing to send short stories, poetry, plays, and other wildly unremunerative genres out into the world.

I'm incredibly lucky to have as my editor and friend the exceptionally astute Jessica Grant, who nudges and probes until she feels a story is right, who notices things no one else would, who possesses a finely tuned appreciation for the little weirdnesses of the world. If Pulitzer prizes were awarded for beautifully written editor's notes, which they should be, Jessica would have won. She is a true Olympian.

Many thanks to Marianne Ward for her assiduous copy editing.

Lisa Moore has been reading these stories in bits and pieces ever since I started writing them. Without her, the book would never have been finished. Also, annoyingly, she has been right about very many things. I have learned an enormous amount by reading her work.

My husband, Larry Mathews, has offered invaluable feedback and saved me from the odd disastrous misstep. My children, Tim and Sal Mathews, have opened windows into worlds I would not otherwise have discovered. I am indebted to my parents for bringing me up in a house full of books and encouraging me to read them. Love you all.

Eric (E. R.) Brown, Diane Collier, Libby Creelman, and Ramona Dearing have commented thoughtfully on individual stories.

The current members of the Burning Rock writing group— Libby Creelman, Ramona Dearing, Jack Eastwood, Mark Ferguson, Larry Mathews, Lisa Moore, and Beth Ryan— are a remarkable bunch of people. I am inspired by their work, excited by their ideas and so very glad to have them as friends.

AUTHOR PHOTO: MICHAEL WILKSHIRE

CLAIRE WILKSHIRE is a writer and editor living in St. John's with her husband, writer Larry Mathews. They have two adult children.

The Love Olympics is Claire's first story collection. Her short fiction has also appeared in *Grain*, the *New Quarterly*, *Event*, the *Fiddlehead*, and elsewhere. *Maxine*, a novel, was published by Breakwater in 2013. Claire is a member of the Burning Rock writing group.